Mrs. George Linnaeus Banks

Ripples and Breakers

A volume of verse

Mrs. George Linnaeus Banks

Ripples and Breakers
A volume of verse

ISBN/EAN: 9783337105457

Printed in Europe, USA, Canada, Australia, Japan

Cover: Foto ©Andreas Hilbeck / pixelio.de

More available books at **www.hansebooks.com**

RIPPLES AND BREAKERS.

Front.

RIPPLES AND BREAKERS.

A VOLUME OF VERSE.

BY

Mrs. G. LINNÆUS BANKS,

AUTHORESS OF "GOD'S PROVIDENCE HOUSE," "THE MANCHESTER MAN,"
"DAISIES IN THE GRASS" (CONJOINTLY WITH MR. BANKS), ETC.

ILLUSTRATED BY JOHN PROCTOR AND G. C. BANKS.

LONDON.:
C. KEGAN PAUL & CO., 1, PATERNOSTER SQUARE.
1878.

CONTENTS.

CONTENTS.

CONTENTS.

LEGENDARY.

" Waves of thought,

RIPPLES AND BREAKERS.

"INDUSTRIA ET PROBITATE." *

(TO MY SON.)

UR ancestor at Hastings fought,
    A Norman baron, clad in mail ;
    And on his shield and scarf were
      wrought
    A motto ne'er by bloodshed
      bought ;
Yet valour had its spirit caught,
      And in the fight
      That armèd knight
Felt every blow was for the right,
    And being right could never
      fail ;
It nerved his arm for victory
By " Industry and Probity."

---

* The motto of the Varley family, to
which the writer belongs.

Scorn not the motto as unmeet
   For feudal times and battle-cry;
For fields where fiery foemen greet
The ringing axe with iron sleet,
And tread out lives with bloody feet
      Intent to slay!
      Sure in such fray
Some consciousness of right must sway
   The leaders who thus dare to die!
And golden spurs to victory
Are " Industry and Probity."

Those feudal times have passed away,
   Earldom and barony are gone,
Castle and lands own other sway—
Forfeit for treason, so they say;
Not e'en to us remains to-day
      The right to bear
      Their 'scutcheon fair,
For rights like these with wealth decay;
   And even my birth-name is gone.
Yet cling I with tenacity
To "Industry and Probity."

We fight far other battles now,
   No kingly quarrels ask our aid;

Yet every manly heart and brow
Is scarred in fight as fierce, I trow ;
And whether pencil, pen, or plough
　　　Be ours to wield,
　　　Our surest shield
In struggling on, all will allow,
　Is conscious right and earnest zeal ;
And so, my son, hold sturdily
By " Industry and Probity."

'Tis all our ancestors have left
　To mark their course in field or town ;
Whether through serried ranks they cleft,
Or drove the dagger to the heft,
And the fierce stag of life bereft,
　　　Or battered wall
　　　Echoed the call
First shouted by some craftsman deft,
　Who, fighting, won his mural crown ;
Yet a right noble legacy
Is " Industry and Probity."

So, guard within thy inmost heart
　That Norman's cry, howe'er attained ;
Assured that no ignoble part
Was played in battle, field, or mart,
By him who wrote upon his chart

That worthy line.
So make it thine;
Hold up the words like stars to shine
Upon a life by vice unstained;
And fight thy battle trenchantly
By "Industry and Probity."

BEATING AGAINST THE BARS.

WHAT would I give to end the restless strife
      Which men call life ?
To reach unchallenged the celestial goal
      Of the freed soul?
What would I give ?   Ah, me ! what have I to resign
      I can call mine?

Beauty ?—Scant dower of loveliness was mine, forsooth,
      Even in youth ;
And the small gifts were called back one by one,
      Till all were gone.
Now ;—what of beauty could the passer-by
      In me descry ?

Youth ?—With its proud resolves, high hopes and schemes,
      Its glad day-dreams ;—
Youth,—looking up intent on the " still higher,"
      Full of strange fire,
Of life, and health, and energy to *do*—
      Thou art gone too !

Wealth ?—That did aye elude my timid clasp.
                    I had no strength to grasp,
No magic net to catch the golden spoil
                    With little toil :
The mintage of the brain and of the mart
          ·   Are far apart.

Health ?—With full pulses beating steady time
                    To life's best rhyme,
Spirits elastic as the buoyant tread—
                    Thou long hast fled !
My white face mocks my pillow, my thin hand
                    Drops down like sand.

Love ?—I had a heart-shaped chalice brimmed with wine
                    From fount of thine.
I gave my goblet, bubbling richly up,
                    For a like cup :—
I bartered wine for water and sour lees.
                    Is *love* of *these ?*

I would give much—but what ?—for leave to fade away
                    Out of this clay.
I have nor Beauty, Youth, nor Wealth to render up,
                    Nor Love's full cup,
Nor Health's pure balsam.   I have nought to bring
                    As offering.

Let me be patient, since in each heart-beat
    I hear the feet
Of the sure messenger who comes to all
    With mystic pall :
But louder still, a voice in solemn tones
    Rebukes my moans :—

" Oh, panting heart ! chafe not with fluttering rage
    Against thy cage :—
For *others*, not for self, God gave thee place
    In life's sharp race.
The pulse may ebb, feet bleed—but *duty done*,
    The goal is won ! "

SUNSHINE ON THE SEA.

THERE are blossoms on the cherry,
    There is bloom upon the pear,
    And my heart is light and merry
       With the hope that blossoms there ;
For the sorrow and the weeping
  Wintry tempests brought to me
In the past are calmly sleeping :—
  Now there's sunshine on the sea.
I am looking for my lover,
  Who is true as truth to me,
Now the winter storms are over
  And there's sunshine on the sea.

" When the bloom of pear and cherry
  Are white upon the tree—
When you see the bud and berry,
  Then look out, my love, for me ; "

So he said, when last we parted,
  While my tears rained on the deck ;
For I felt half broken-hearted
  In my dread of storm and wreck.
Now, each spring-tide bud and blossom
  Brings my own love nearer me,
And the sunshine in my bosom
  Is the sunshine on the sea.

ONLY A WORD.

FRIVOLOUS word, a sharp retort,
   A parting in angry haste,—
The sun that rose on a bower of bliss,
The loving look, and the tender kiss,
   Has set on a barren waste,
Where pilgrims tread, with weary feet,
Paths destined never more to meet.

A frivolous word, a sharp retort,
   A moment that blots out years,—
Two lives are wrecked on a stormy shore,
Where billows of passion surge and roar
   To break in a spray of tears ;
Tears shed to blind the severed pair
Drifting seaward and drowning there.

A frivolous word, a sharp retort,
   A flash from a passing cloud,—
Two hearts are scathed to their inmost core,
Are ashes and dust for evermore ;
   Two faces turn to the crowd,

Masked by pride with a life-long lie,
To hide the scars of that agony.

A frivolous word, a sharp retort,
  An arrow at random sped,—
It has cut in twain the mystic tie
That had bound two souls in harmony ;
  Sweet love lies bleeding or dead.
A poisoned shaft, with scarce an aim,
Has done a mischief sad as shame.

A frivolous word, a sharp retort,—
  Alas ! for the loves and lives
So little a cause has rent apart ;
Tearing the fondest heart from heart
  As a whirlwind rends and rives ;
Never to reunite again,
But live and die in secret pain.

A frivolous word, a sharp retort,—
  Alas ! that it should be so ;
The petulant speech, the careless tongue,
Have wrought more evil and done more wrong,
  Have brought to the world more woe,
Than all the armies age to age
Records on history's blood-stained page.

THE MYSTERY OF LIFE'S BATTLE.

I AM looking, yes, am looking with sad eyes that
    see not yet,
    What there can be worth the brooking in this
world of cark and fret ;
I am peering, dull of hearing, through the mist and through
    the sound,
For the reason of the cheering that ariseth all around.

I hear neighing, I hear braying from the trumpet's clamorous
    throat ;
See the warriors' dread arraying, hear the cannon's thund'rous
    note ;
See the flashing, hear the clashing of the swords that meet
    and smite ;
Hear the crimson torrent splashing through the darkness
    and the light.

I hear moaning, I hear groaning, I hear hoof-beats on the
    plain—
Chargers trampling (no one owning) on the living and the
    slain ;

I hear wailing unavailing o'er the dying and the dead,
See the widow's cold lips paling as she lifts a gory head.

I see traces on all faces of a battle lost and won;
Ask, "Whom victory disgraces? What the gain when all
is done?"
I hear "Glory, glory, glory!" for an answer 'mid the din,—
That old and worn-out story—as if murder were not sin!

And I ponder, as I wander o'er the battle-field of Life,
On all the good we squander in its everlasting strife;
All the sadness and the madness of the universal creed,
That, for one man's gain or gladness, it is needful many
bleed.

If unspoken, still the token of this faith lies all around;
Though silence be not broken, there is language without
sound;
And the rattle of the battle, in the pulpit, on the mart,
In boudoirs where women prattle, is enough to rend the heart.

Statesmen palter, pastors falter, as they bend to power and
might,
Or lay down on self's high altar every sense of shame and
right;
And the clerkly, penning darkly what seem facts for public
eyes,
Do not scruple to give starkly the most flagitious lies.

Now I shiver by the river whose dark bridges, long and
 wide,
Tell of gasping sob and quiver, and the splash beneath
 the tide;
Of the mortal at that portal which opens inwards only;—
Where Mercy waits—immortal—for the suffering and lonely.

Vigils keeping, worn with weeping, with gaunt famine, toil,
 or care,
While soft Luxury lies sleeping, I see women young and fair;
Dusty treadle, rusty needle, idle spindle, silent loom,
Call to sexton and to beadle, "Find this stricken 'surplus'
 room."

But while looking, sadly looking, with my eyes all dim and
 wet,
If aught be worth the brooking in this world of cark and
 fret,
A bright angel, whose evangel is to open ears and eyes,
Tears the veil from many a strange ill I behold beneath the
 skies.

I see evils which grim devils have sown broadcast on the
 earth
As food for fiendish revels, bear some fruit of nobler birth:
Pity faintly, pure and saintly, lulls the wounded unto rest;
While Benevolence, robed quaintly, breaks the chain of the
 oppressed.

In dim alleys, at the galleys, both by want and crime
accurst,
With a foot that never dallies, comes sweet Charity the first :
She aye chases from foul places fell Despair's envenomed
brood,
And warms ice-cold hearts and faces with the flame of
Gratitude.

Falsehood's vassal, drunk with wassail, may uprear his
standard black,
But still Truth maintains her castle, having Courage at her
back ;
Not a sorrow but can borrow a sun-ray from Faith and
Hope,
And Fortitude's to-morrow lies beyond our human scope.

Then the rattle of Life's battle had significance for me,
As I saw Good born of Evil was God's sacred mystery.
Thus enlightened, my eye brightened, for I felt that earth
was fair,
And I turned to thank the angel—he had vanished into
air !

THE BIRD ON THE LINDEN.

A LITTLE bird sang on a linden tree
    In the balmy days of spring,
      When his lay of love woke a voice in me,
  And *I* essayed to sing :
The song of the bird was jocund and glad
  As song of a bird might be,
My answering strain was mournful and sad
  As I sat 'neath that linden tree.

For close by the bird on the linden tree
  Sat a mate with folded wing,
But never a mate was there for me
  To listen whilst I might sing :
My spring was past, and my life was lone,
  Love never had beamed on me—
I could not echo the joyous tone
  Of that bird on the linden tree.

The little bird sang on the linden tree
  When summer was warm and bright,
And now I could answer his minstrelsy
  With a song of deep delight.
For the heart I had long despaired to gain
  Had blossomed with love for me.
Oh, joy ! *we* were one, who before were twain—
  And we sat 'neath the linden tree.

OH, SAY!

OH, say, has the tremulous snowdrop
    Rung its bells o'er the frozen mould?
    Or the crocus arrayed its lances
As a guard for the cup of gold?
Or timorous eye of the daisy
    Peeped out from her veil of grass,
To inquire if the Spring be coming,
    From the courier winds that pass?

Oh, say, are the tree-buds swelling
    With a promise of future leaves?
Do the young birds seem to be courting
    Or building beneath the eaves?
Have the breezes or sunbeams whispered,
    "Surly Winter has ceased to reign?"
Do the brooks run along rejoicing
    To escape from his icy chain?

I long for a token of springtide
Beyond that of lengthening light ;
I would fain see an early daisy,
Or a snowdrop so pure and white :
I have lain so long on my pillow,
My soul had so nigh taken wing,
I yearn for the perfume and promise
That come with the blooms of the Spring.

THE KINGSHIP OF THE SEA.

On the night of October 7th, 1799, H.M.S. *Lutine*, freighted with several millions of specie, foundered off the sandbanks on the coast of Holland. The *Lutine* contained, likewise, the crown jewels of Holland, which had been sent to London for resetting. These were packed in an hermetically sealed strong iron case. The specie was partly subsidy money for troops, partly assignments to bankers and bullion-dealers. Only one person escaped to tell the story of the wreck. The sunken vessel lay about three leagues from shore, at times accessible to divers, at times hidden by drifting sands. Many projects were set on foot at long intervals to recover the treasure ; some portions were obtained, but disasters and litigation put a stop to further attempts. In 1869 a fresh project was afoot for the recovery of the treasure, by means of immense iron caissons to be sunk in the sand, and surround the skeleton ship as with a dry dock, little doubt being entertained of the result.

IN thy insatiate maw,
O Sea, lie treasures rare !
Open thy foamy jaw,
Lay thy brown bosom bare,
As soon thou must !
The *Lutine* lies a wreck
Beneath thy angry tides ;
Thy currents sweep her deck
And beat her oaken sides,
So true to trust.

It is no common prize
    Thou holdest in thy grip;
A regal treasure lies
    Hid in that sunken ship,
        Low in the brine.
Within thy miser hold
    Men's *souls* thou couldst not keep,
But o'er rich gems and gold
    Thy slimy fingers creep
        As they were thine.

Long hast thou leapt and raved
    Exultant o'er thy spoil,
And weedy banners waved
    Derisive of our toil,
        Thou thievish Main !
Laughing, with boist'rous glee,
    As each defeated band
Relinquished hopelessly,
    To tides and drifting sand,
        Our gold and slain !

Hadst thou not wrought this ill,
    On princely brow and breast
These gems had sparkled still ;
    And for each seaman's rest,
        Time made a grave.

Now, shake thy locks with spleen ;
   Once more we seek our own :
Science will sit serene
   On thy invaded throne,
     King of the wave !

Thine was the right of strength ;—
   Thou hast that right no more ;
Thou must resign at length
   The casket and its store
     To human skill.
Science has probed the deep
   To lay the *Lutine* bare ;
Where now thy waters sweep
   Will rush the fluent air,
     Man's servant still.

We are the victors now,
   Will wrest our own from thee,
And many a sunken prow
   Raise from the lapping sea
     In every clime.
We warn thee that thy reign
   Is well-nigh overpast ;
Sole monarch of the main
   Science will be' at last,
     Through future time.

Hark ! What replies the Sea ?
" I laugh your threats to scorn ;
The conqueror of me
Is yet of the unborn
'Mongst mortal men !
Can Science bar the wind,
Smooth the Atlantic waves,
Or give the human kind
Entombed in ocean caves
Their life again ?

" Can Science name or count
The creatures in my train,
Or reckon the amount
Of treasures in the main—
Tell form or tint ?
Can Science take a chart
Of iceberg or drifting floe,
Or tell upon the mart
Where my coral islands grow,
As hard as flint ?

" Can Science build a bark
I have not power to wreck,
Or make the hungry shark
Submissive to its beck ?—
Then,—not till then,

Must Science boast its sway
  Or claim my kingly crown,
Though for once I deign to lay
  My potent sceptre down
    To pleasure men.

" What though I may resign
  The *Lutine's* coinèd gold,
Give its jewels back to shine
  For princes as of old ;—
    I still am King !
What though I grant to man
  A league or so from shore ;
What though his cables span
  My bed for evermore ;—
    I still am King !

" Man cannot quell my storms,
  He cannot bind me fast,
Or save his fairest forms
  When I wrestle with the blast —
    So I am King !
He cannot wipe the froth
  From my foamy upper-lip,
When I curl it in my wrath
  O'er doomèd town or ship ;—
    So I am King !

" Potent for good or ill,
Potent to bless or ban,
Yielding to Science still
Whate'er is good for man ;
But *as* a King !
For King I must remain
Till Time shall no more be,
'Till the dead shall rise again,
And there be no more sea,
And but *One King !*"

MY INKSTAND.

"LITTLE vessel, black and grim,
Filled with fluid to the brim,
What hold'st thou in thy brass-bound rim?"

"Ink I hold for thee and thine,
Ink for ode or valentine,
Laundry list or strain divine.

"Ink, with gall to tip the pen;
Black, to smirch the fame of men;
Water, to wash white again.

"Ink, but more than ink, I hold,—
Thoughts to bring thee fame and gold,
Words to give the thoughts a mould.

"Fancies subtle, keen, and bright,
Lie within me hid from sight:
Dip thy pen and give them light.

" Waters sparkling, fresh, and clear ;
Flowers that fade not all the year ;
Love that never cost a tear ;

" Youth that knoweth not decay ;
Auburn locks that turn not grey ;
Rainbows that for ever stay ;

" Tapestry from fairy loom ;
Beauty with perennial bloom ;
Glory shutting out the tomb ;

" Countless mines of gems and gold ;
Friends who never can grow cold ;
Statesmen never bought or sold ;

" Honour that was never stained ;
Sons who mothers never pained ;
Better kings than ever reigned ;

" Poets who o'ertopped their aim ;
Fadeless wreaths for after-fame ;
Rays to gild a simple name ;

" All that fancy can conceive,
All that wildest fiction weave,
To delight or to deceive,

" Lie within my brass-bound rim,
Black, unpromising, and grim,
Crude, chaotic, vague, and dim.

" Ink, and *only* ink to men
Of common mould and common ken,
With common uses for the pen ;

" But, to the gifted ones of earth,
Familiar with my secret worth,
An essence of immortal birth ! "

WHO ARE "THE PEOPLE"?

THE rogues who drink, and fight, and curse,
    Who take a life to steal a purse,
      Still driving on from bad to worse?
        These cannot be the People !
Who beat their women, miscalled wives,
And, foul with crime that never thrives,
Blot love from out their children's lives?
        These roughs are not the People !

The dainty fops who stroll the Mall,
Or idly haunt boudoir and ball,
The club, the Row, the opera-stall?
        Loungers are not the People !
The worse than fops who spend the night
In vices which profane the light,
And think indulgence theirs by right?
        Roués are not the People !

All they of deft or horny hand
Who in the mill or workshop stand,
Or dig our mines, or till our land ;—
      Say, are not these the People ?
All they who strive with heart and will
Their humble duty to fulfil,
And earn an honest living still ;—
      Sure, these must be the People ?

Nay ;—they who toil with hands alone,
To forge our metal, hew our stone—
Merely machines of flesh and bone—
      Can but be half a People !
But they—whate'er their class or state—
Whose minds control, whose minds create,
Whose hands and heads make nations great ;
      These thinkers are the People !

Yes,—they who work, and they who plan
To elevate and better man,
Conjoined may press into the van
      And say, " We are the People !"
But mere brute force, mere wealth, mere birth,
Cannot regenerate the earth ;
'Tis thought *and* action, work *and* worth,
      Combined, that make a People !

QUARR ABBEY.

RUIN grey, in a tangled nook,
    Nestles where ripples a silver rill,
    Singing sweet songs out of Nature's book
To the ferns at the foot of a daisied hill.
Ages have flown since the abbey bell
    Rang out for matin or midnight prayer,
And barely a legend remains to tell
    Of the monks ascetic who flourished there.

Chancel and nave have crumbled away,
    Nor shrine nor altar remaineth now,.
Yet worshippers still come here to pray,
    And trust the walls with the whispered vow.
Maidens come hither, and not alone,
    Nor yet as students in ancient lore;
They listen to more than the brooklet's tone
    Or stories of monks and nuns of yore.

Taught by the song of the rippling brook,
  Yearnings unspoken a voice will find,
To win from the maiden an answering look
  And the word of fate two loves to bind.
Yet never a monkish ghost dare rise,
  To censure love's consecrating kiss ;
The rill-kissed fern alone replies
  With an envious sigh at the newer bliss.

And straight from the rill and the ruins grey
  The plighted lovers pass into the world ;
Some to marry, and some to stray
  In paths where no frond of fern is unfurled ;
But the rippling rill, and the tangled nook,
  Quarr's ancient abbey, and daisied hill,
Will fill a page in memory's book,
  Blotted with tears, or smiled on still.

AH, ME!

 MEASURE life by gravestones, not by years ;
    They are the milestones on my life's highway ;
For rain of heaven they have been wet with tears—
        Are wet to-day !

Tears of the heart, not of the clouded eye,
    Bedew these sepulchres of blighted blooms,
Where, unresponsive, the beloved ones lie
        In far-off tombs.

Dear friends, who journeyed with me hand in hand,
    And dropped, way-worn, leaving sad me behind,
To seek alone that bright and better land
        Faith looks to find.

My baby-buds, sweet blossoms of my love,
    With sentient leaves expanding day by day ;
Whose essence envious Death exhaled above,
        And left me—clay.

Fair human forms surrendered to the dust,
　My human tears may dew *your* verdant graves ;
But there are buried hopes—uncoffined trusts—
　　　　Where no grass waves.

There will be "resurrection of the dead ;"
　Parted humanity expects to meet
All smiles and love—where never tears are shed—
　　　　In bliss complete.

Some hopes died early, others in their prime,
　And the heart shrouds them in a viewless pall ;
But *they* will rise not in the after-time
　　　　At *any* call.

I measure life by gravestones, not by years ;
　And these, intangible, count with the seen ;
The dead hopes buried in a rain of tears—
　　　　The "should have been."

And not I only—for, alas ! all men
　Inurn dead hopes within their secret souls,
But seldom mark their graves for mortal ken
　　　　With open scrolls.

MY MOTHER'S OLD SHOE.

(A CITY MERCHANT'S RETROSPECT.)

" REMEMBER the parting from mother and home
In the time long ago, ere my fortune had come:
My years were but few, and my pocket was light,
Whilst the world lay before me to use as I might.
The parting was hopeful, yet anxious and sore,
And my mother's old shoe followed me from the door,
With a blessing so fervent, so tender, so true,
I felt there was luck in the cast of that shoe.

" I think my steps faltered at first on the track,
But I set my face forward and never looked back;
I'd a purpose before me I could not resign,
Though the tears wet my cheeks for that mother of mine,
Whose earnest advice lingers yet on my mind,
For it came like a psalm on the breath of the wind:
' Love mercy, act justly, walk humbly, be true,
And my blessing shall follow you with my old shoe.'

" I had roamed o'er our mountains, gazed out on the sea,
Till the bounds of our vale grew too narrow for me;
And I felt there were cities and places beyond
Where men need not stagnate like weeds in a pond;
Where was work for the seeking, and gold to be won,
And the son need not end where the father begun.
So I made up my mind, bade the farmstead 'adieu,'
And was followed with blessings and mother's old shoe.

" I trudged forward stoutly, and rode when I could,
For my means would not let me do just as I would :
I was bound to be frugal and husband my store,
Since my journey would end at no welcoming door.
And each city and town I went through, or went past,
Made me feel myself little—the wilderness vast;
And my boy's heart sank low when came London in
    view,
Till I thought of the omen of mother's old shoe.

" Long I traversed the city, employment to gain;
But, unknown and unfriended, 'twas hard to obtain,
With no recommendation from any 'last place,'
Save that writ by God on an honest lad's face.
Yet this seemed no passport where'er I applied,
Men doubted the worth that had never been tried :
When—disheartened, despairing—hope sprang up anew
With a cast of good luck from my mother's old shoe.

"At last one man trusted my face or my tone—
Took me in, found me work, made my dwelling his own.
How I served is best told by the progress I made
From that lowly first step up the ladder of trade.
But promotion is certain when duty is done,
And I never swerved from the course once begun;
'Love mercy, act justly, walk humbly, be true,'
Being graved as a motto on mother's old shoe.

"Resolved to be rich in my manhood and age,
From the first I was prudent, and saved from my wage,
Kept free from the pleasures which lure into crime,
And husbanded surely the 'small change' of time.
Such books as bring knowledge I carefully read,
And made myself wiser while sloth lay abed.
Then I loved—not too wisely—as seldom men do,—
But I think I went wooing without the old shoe.

"All went smoothly until came the sordid rebuff
To my heart's earnest suit—I was 'not rich enough.'
Love, honesty, industry, scarce worth a thought,
And my own thriving business, too, counted as nought.
That reply set a seal on my bachelor life,
And I turned unto commerce as unto a wife,
Coming back to my traffic with vigour anew,
Yet regarding the precept on mother's old shoe.

" Then fortune smiled on me when threatened with loss :
I'd an offer—and took it—the ocean to cross ;
For self and for others commissioned to act
In a delicate case asking prudence and tact.
Heavy sums were at stake—but I brought back the gold,
And a knowledge to me worth the cash seven-fold,—
What our colonists needed—then known but to few ;
So I sent future shipments in mother's old shoe.

" From that time all prospered—I gave without stint,
Yet gold poured upon me as if from a mint.
I bought the old homestead I left in my youth,
Where I learned to love virtue, and honour, and truth :
I gathered around me my kith and my kin,
Setting them in the way a like fortune to win ;
And I strove to walk humbly, still keeping in view
The precept engraved on my mother's old shoe.

" Men marry, and then their hearts narrow, no doubt,
To the small sphere of home, and the circle about ;
But I've felt mine expand with the growth of my purse,
And open to all under poverty's curse ;
I've lifted the falling, and helped in their need
The struggling and suff'ring, regardless of creed.
But what my right hand did my left never knew;
I read better the motto on mother's old shoe.

"That mother who would have been proud of her son,
Had she but lived to see the position he won ;
The name upon 'Change now as good as the best,
And the good-will to men put so oft to the test.
I recall how she spoke of my progress with pride,
When I went in my manhood to sit by her side,
And pay to the last all the reverence due
To the mother whose blessing so hallowed her shoe.

"My mother's old shoe ! All I am, or have been,
I trace back to its source in that one parting scene,
When I left the old homestead, untutored, untried,
For a world full of pitfalls both open and wide,
With little to steady my upward career,
Save the blessing which lingered so long on my ear.
And when men call me *lucky*, as thoughtless men do,
I think of that blessing, and mother's old shoe !"

THE HERALD OF SUMMER.

 HEAR a gush of melody, I see a flush of green,
So I know the Summer's coming, with the glory
of a queen;
For Spring, her welcome herald, has proclaimed it far and
wide,
Since the throne of Winter toppled, and the stern old despot
died.

Spring has spread o'er moor and mountain a carpet for her
feet,
Silver daisy, golden king-cup, purple orchis, cowslip sweet;
Bade the trees unfold a canopy of undulating shade,
Where anemone and violet their woodland home have
made.

Pale narcissus and faint daffodil whisper of her by the well,
Where ferns bend o'er the primrose lest she the secret tell;
But hyacinth and harebell ring the tidings boldly out,
For the breeze to catch the echoes, and answer with a shout.

The busy brooklets, listening, have turned the theme to song,
And sing it to the sedges as they gently glide along;
The mountain streams, no longer dumb, join in the joyous
    lay,
And leaping o'er their rocky bounds laugh out in sparkling
    spray.

Glad butterflies are fluttering like banners in the air;
Rich flowers hold up their nectaries and offer incense rare;
The toiling bee hums cheerily, the gnats dance in the sun;
The very frogs croak gleefully o'er springtide life begun.

No need the tardy cuckoo's note to gossip of the spring,
Whilst other warblers' tuneful throats have a prophetic ring;
And orchards white with cherry-snow, through which blooms
     apple-blush,
Bring dreams of summer fruitage to the birdlings in the bush.

Spring is here! and Summer's coming, with a coronal of
    light,
For the skylark, like a courtier, has winged his upward flight,
The first to meet Queen Summer in her golden car of state,
And salute her with his anthem close to her palace gate.

OF AGE!

(TO MY NEPHEW H. E. W., FEBRUARY 5, 1870.)

F age! The simple striking of a clock
Has changed the youth to man! A point
of time,
A few vibrations of a pendulum,
A leap from prison walls to liberty,
A bound from vassalage to monarchy,
Subject at once, and king! Like magic freed
From that parental rule enforced by law,
And left amenable alone to love.

Of age! Twenty-one years ago, a wail
Proclaimed a man-child born into the world:
To-day a *man* is born—a thinking man,
Responsible to God and to his fellows
For use of life: responsible to law
For use of liberty: yet free to act,

To come and go at will, as impulse prompts
Or reason dictates. 'Tis a thoughtful time,
Since putting off the boy brings manhood's cares ;
And the world weights them heavily to all.

But buoyant Hope comes in with beaming face
And sows life's future field with promises :
The harvest is to come. Yet from the past
A voice prophetic rings—"So good a son,
So kind a brother, and so true a friend,
So just a servant, too, must needs do well !"
Home blessings fill thy sails, and so thy bark
May breast life's waters gallantly, and bring
Its freight of aims and projects into port
In after time. My feeble breath,
Praying a prosperous voyage unto thee,
May help to swell the sails. God speed thee on !
Have Christ for pilot—Virtue at the helm—
The Bible for thy chart,—then dread no storms
Or shipwreck by the way.

CHANT OF STORM WINDS.

COME, brothers, come; haste o'er the sea,
    Lashing its waves to foam;
    An army of bodiless spirits are we,
      Ever through space we roam—
    Ever, ever, pausing never,
    Sweeping onwards, ever, ever!

    Up go the waves, up to the skies,
      Clouds scud over the moon;
Down, down sink the billows, and up again rise,
      With wild and angry tune;
    Restless ever, pausing never,
    Madly surging, ever, ever!

    Mark, as we rush, huge vessels reel
      Quiv'ring like paper boats:
The stout ship may shudder from capstan to keel,
      Care we if she sinks or floats!
    Ever, ever, pausing never,
    Fateful brothers we are ever!

The helmsman feels our blinding hair
    Drifting across his face,
But he sees not the talons that rive and tear
    In our destructive chase ;
    Pressing onwards, pausing never,
    Felt though viewless, ever, ever !

We snap the cordage, rend the mast,
    Flapping to shreds each sail,
Till the mariner sobs to the sobbing blast
    From a wreck before the gale ;
    Fiercely flying, pausing never,
    Swooping landwards, onwards ever !

Earth hears the rushing of our wings,
    And trembles as we pass ;
For we crush the pride of material things
    As men's feet crush the grass ;
    Restless ever, pausing never,   .
    Storm winds, weird and mighty ever !

Titanic trees we rend in twain,
    Whirl roofs like flakes of snow,
Swirl mortals like motes in our mad hurricane,
    And castles like cards o'erthrow ;
    Ever, ever, pausing never,
    Potent spirits, dreaded ever !

Sin shudders at our voices wild
　　As we rush howling past ;
Men stalwart and burly, whom guilt hath defiled,
　　Crouch 'neath the searching blast,
　　Piercing ever, pausing never,
　　Slumb'ring conscience rousing ever !

Lost spirits, agonized with pain,
　　To our earth-bound brothers
Shrieking this summons to join our wild train—
　　" Ye are ours, and we Another's ; "
　　Ever, ever, pausing never,
　　Calling souls to us for ever !

Storm spirits, working wreck and woe
　　With devastating breath ;
Our ban may bring blessings we never may know
　　Though hand in hand with death ;
　　Ever, spite our fierce endeavour,
　　To *His* will subdued for ever !

On, brothers, on ; with wings unfurled ;
　　Dreaded, not understood ;
We are driving pestilence out of the world,
　　Working not ill, but good ;
　　Ever, spite our fierce endeavour,
　　God's own ministers for ever !

HARK!

HARK !—I listen with hands on my breast,
    To still the beat of my heart.
      Oh, rustling leaves ! for an instant rest ;
And, bird, keep silence within your nest ;—
    I am waiting with lips apart.

Old tree, thou never canst thrill as I
    With hope and expectancy ;
Yet your leaflets flutter when breezes sigh,
As if a lover were drawing nigh,
    And so thou mayst feel for me.

Birdie, singing of love to thy mate,
    Knowest thou nought of the pain
To listen trembling, to watch and wait,
To feel each moment is full of fate,
    To look for the loved in vain ?

E

Oh, linnet and leaves ! be quiet awhile,
 And list for my love with me ;
I shall hear his foot ere he crosses the stile,
And know if he bring me a tear or a smile,
 So vocal his step to me.

Hark ! he is coming—— Ah, no, not yet !
 Oh, tremulous heart, be still!
He will not, cannot his word forget,
Is sure to be here ere the sun has set,
 If he love me, I know he will !

Bird, thy jubilant carol restrain,
 For my pulse beats out of tune,—
My temples ache with a leaden pain :
What if he ne'er should meet me again ?—
 Love die ere its perfect noon?

Hark ! he is coming, he *is* coming now !
 How foolish my fears have been !
Let me smooth my hair from my flushing brow,
And, bird, sing out from thy leafy bough,
 For joy comes with him, I ween !

OUR BIRTHDAYS.

S seasons come and seasons go,
　　We mark their passage thus :—
　　First buds, then leafage, fruitage, snow ;
And so the cycles round and grow,
　　And mark their sum on us.

Ay, all the ages that have flown
　　Since Adam saw the sun
Have marked their impress on our own ;
And we when babes are fuller grown
　　Than he when life was done.

And, born into an older world,
　　A philosophic race,
We have Time's coiled-up scroll uncurled,
Rent Earth's green veil, with tears impearled,
　　To scan her wrinkled face.

We say these wrinkles represent
    Æons of ages gone ;
And, in our wisdom self-content,
Proclaim how strata, reft and rent,
    Are birthdays stamped in stone.

And, busied tracing back the growth
    Of this terraqueous sphere,
Is it forgetfulness, or sloth,
That makes us yearly grow more loth
    To count our birthday's here ?

Ah, no !   In youth we sprang to greet
    Each birthday as it came,
Until—maturity complete—
Years seemed to run with racing feet,
    And bear a cross of flame.

We feel not, whilst fresh seasons pass,
    Their footfalls on the brow,
Until some clear unflattering glass
Reveals the wrinkles, which, alas !
    Are furrowed by their plough.

And as those furrows indicate
  The throes of strife or pain,
The heart that was with love elate
In age bends 'neath too sad a weight
  Its birthdays to sustain.

What marvel we pass mournfully
  Remembrancers of care,
Epochs of mutability,
Of passion, strife, or agony,
  If such our birthdays were?

IN LANGUID JUNE.

IS pleasant to stroll by the unruffled stream
    When June's fervid sun seeks the crimsoning
      west,
And leisurely look on each lingering beam
  So softly caressing the bird on its nest;
To know that the glare of the noontide is past,
    That purple clouds steal o'er the crest of the hill,
The smith's clanging hammer will soon be downcast,
    And silence o'ershadow forge, ferry, and mill.

'Tis pleasant to feel that the weary old beast
    Now dragging the dull barge so lazily on
Will soon from his harness and toil be released,
    Most thankful the sultry day's duty is done;
Afar off to hear the last swish of the scythe,
    To scent the sweet odours that come from the hay,
And see the tired haymakers laughing and blithe
    Abandon the meadow for rest or for play.

When bees, flocking homeward, forsake the rich blooms,
  And hollyhocks offer their nectar in vain,
'Tis sweet to throw work by and leave our close rooms
  To breathe the fresh air in the perfumed green lane ;
Thence stray to the river, and close to the brink
  To gather ripe grasses, forget-me-nots blue,
And flushed with the stooping, rise slowly to think,
  Of loved ones home-coming, to me and to you.

THE GIANT'S LIMBS.

(AS SEEN FROM A SUBURBAN WINDOW.)

SWEEP the wide horizon with mine eye,
      And what behold?
The vast expanse of canopying sky
      All blue and gold ;
The distant woods, a chequered wall of green,
Lie on my left ; masts on the right are seen
Dwindled to wands meet for a fairy queen.

Betwixt, the line is broken by tall spires,
      And, taller still,
Chimneys, with tongues of smoke to tell of fires
      That do man's will
On wood or metal, fibres coarse or fine,
Changing black refuse into hues divine,
Or stamping thought on paper—as *thus* mine.

Nearer intrudes a railway blank and harsh,
　　　　Yet cannot bar
The prospect of the river and the marsh,
　　　　Or ait afar,
Where groups of pliant poplars, straight and slim,
Trembling, protest against invasion grim
From bricks and mortar which their glories dim.

I fain would sweep into the river's bed
　　　　Yon solid screen
Of hideous brick-work, with its roof of red ;—
　　　　It mars the scene,
Breathes tarry vapours to pollute the gale,
Shuts almost from my sight the gliding sail,
Though not the flying vampire of the rail.

Well may those ancient poplars groan and bend,
　　　　As, round a grave
Stand mourners, loth to leave some dear dead friend
　　　　They could not save ;
They see the *Town* come creeping slowly on,
The green grass going, and the wild flowers gone ;
All nature's beauties dying one by one.

Prophetic thrills must run through root and vein,
　　　　Each quiv'ring leaf
Must to its fellows mutter and complain
　　　　In utter grief,

Lest they, too, should be doomed to pass away
Before the coming giant's foot of clay,
Advancing slowly, surely, day by day.

I see the monster spreading out his arms ;
        And look ahead
To the green woods, still bright with vernal charms,
        To ask, with dread,
If those old trees, the glorious and grand,
Must also fall beneath the spoiler's hand,
And stucco desecrate the sylvan land ?—

If nought can save from Babylonish grip
        Those woodland shades ;
Those bubbling brooks, cool to the eye and lip ;
        Those forest glades,
The gipsy's home from unrecorded times ;
The ferny nooks beneath umbrageous limes,
The choir of birds, the wind-swept harebell's chimes ?

Already hath the keen destroyer's axe
        Polled elm and beech ;
But shall the country suffer such a tax
        And not find speech ?
Shall the encroachment of the Giant Town
Tread unresisted earth's green places down,
And pluck her jewels from the island's crown ?

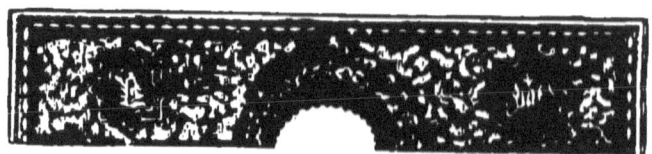

MY SINGING-BIRD.

(A LOVER'S LAY.)

AYE, dreamily warbling from room unto room,
  Or merrily carolling down the broad stair,
  My Eveline passes in maidenly bloom,
Her pure ringing voice floating out on the air
In snatches of melody born in old time,
  When Music herself was as young and as sweet,
That flow from her red lips in confluent chime
  With the rhythmical motion of fingers and feet.

A singing-bird she, with the richest-toned note
  That ever was heard in field, welkin, or wood;
For never did skylark or nightingale's throat
  Blend soul with its song in so perfect a flood;
And whether it falls in a showery spray,
  Like some gushing fountain that breaks in the sun,
Or rolls in a full-tided river away,
  We listen entranced till the minstrel has done.

My Eveline! crowned with the shimmering hair—
　　An aureole meet for the head of a saint,—
There lives not the limner with colour so rare,
　　Or pencil so gifted, thy beauty to paint;
Nor is there a science so subtle can bind
　　The echoes that faint in attempting thy songs—
Those exquisite strains freely flung to the wind,
　　Though the love that inspires to *me only* belongs.

In Eveline all that is graceful and good
　　Meets and blends in one perfect harmonious whole;
And whether be mirthful or mournful my mood,
　　Her song comes responsive—soul answering soul.
So potent the charm of my singing-bird's voice,
　　It quickens my pulse like the flushing of wine;
I hear her, I see her, and trembling rejoice
　　To know that the peerless young songstress is mine.

VEILED.

AT old Egyptian festals, we are told,
    Was aye a guest
Who through the feast sat rigid, silent, cold ;
    Whom no one prest
To share the banquet, yet who still remained
Till the last song was sung, the last cup drained.

The cup, the song, the jest, the laugh went round,
    No cheek turned pale,
No guest amazed did query ere propound,
    Or lift the veil
To learn the wherefore one alone sat mute,
With whom nor host, nor friend, exchanged salute.

Custom and rose-crowned drapery did all :
    That thing of bone,
That hideous skeleton in festal hall,
    Evoked no groan ;
No thrill of horror checked the flow of mirth ;
Unseen, unfelt that grisly type of earth.

But did the host return when all were gone,
      The lights put out,
The unseen presence of that nameless one
      Might put to rout
All the gay fancies born of wine and song,
And speechless dread the fleeting night prolong.

At every hearth, in every human heart
      There sits such guest.
We may not, cannot, bid it thence depart ;
      E'en at the best
We can but crown with roses, veil and drape:
The thing exists though we conceal its shape.

We shroud our skeletons from public gaze,
      And from our own ;
Ignore their presence with life's lamps ablaze,
      Till left alone
With festal fragments, wine-stains, lights gone dim,
We feel them with us, icy, bloodless, grim.

Our nerves would quiver to unveil the bones
      Of the dead past :
We lock them in our hearts, with sighs and moans,
      To keep them fast ;
'Tis but in solitude we turn the key,
And dare to look upon them as they be.

ETHEL.

ETHEL is winsome and wee ;
    Ethel is bonnie and sweet ;
Ethel has two laughing e'e,
    And two pretty capering feet.

Ethel, with fewest of words,
    Few as the pearls they pass through,
Chirrups, as chirrup the birds,
    In tones as incessantly new.

Ethel, the dear little pet,
    Shy as a timorous dove,
Hides, like a finished coquette,
    A face that is beaming with love.

Ethel has budding red lips,
    Tempting the wandering bee ;
Yet must he heed how he sips,
    For, chary of kisses is she.

Ethel, unconscious of theft,
　Innocent, artless and gay,
Yet is surpassingly deft
　At stealing all hearts in her way.

Mine, archly stolen, no doubt,
　Went with a throb like a sigh ;
But Ethel, too loving to pout,
　Will give me her own—by-and-by.

FORGOTTEN.

ILENT, and pale, and clad in white
    (The funeral bell deep tolling),
    Under the screen of the coffin lid
All that was wife and mother lies hid,
Dead,—and buried,—and out of sight,—
    And tears from sad eyes are rolling.

She who was late a home's delight
    (The death-bell scarce done tolling),
Whose virtues live in the fresh-cut stone,
Lies in darkness,—forgotten,—alone,—
Dead,—and buried,—and out of sight,—
    Where tears from the skies are rolling.

Blushing, and glad, and robed in white
    (Blithe wedding bells are pealing),
A bride is led past the still fresh stone
That says in a language all its own,
" Dead and buried—and out of sight !
    Have stones or have hearts more feeling ? "

F

As young and trusting, pure and bright
  (For whom mad bells rang pealing)
As the second-wife he weds to-day,
Was the bride who now is only clay,
Dead,—and buried,—and out of sight
  Of those at the altar kneeling.

The slab bears witness to the light
  (Loud joy-bells o'er it swelling),
Loving motherhood, faith as a wife,
Patient endurance of troublous life,
Dead—and buried—and out of sight,
  Fade as a dream ere the telling.

THE BELL OF ST. BARTHOLOMEW.

THE August sun, with red prophetic eye
    And fiercest noontide ray,
        Rends the cloud-curtains of the angry sky
  This sultry Sabbath day.
Oh, Sabbath ! blessèd God-appointed time
  For peace, and praise, and prayer,
That ever thou shouldst chronicle a crime
  E'en fiends might shrink to share !
France lies in seeming calm, in rest supine,
  When—the loud tocsin clangs,
And the fierce panther of Medici's line,
  Whets her insatiate fangs.
            Boom ! boom !
            It signals doom !

" Down with the Huguenot !" Swords flash to light,
  'Mid shouts, " Kill every man !"
(On breast or sleeve, the scarf or cross of white
  Marks all not under ban) ;

" Down with the Huguenot !"   The swords blush red,
   With blood of man and boy !
" Kill ! kill !"   The bigot hounds, with carnage fed,
   Mother and babe destroy !
Grey hairs protect not ; beauty is no shield ;
   Home ties no longer bind ;
Blood runs down street and stream, stains hearth and field ;
   Shrieks scare the 'bated wind.
              Boom ! boom !
              The knell tolls doom !

The timid stars come out, the moon looks down,
   Then veils her pallid face ;
But stern Medici's sanguinary frown
   Still urges on the chase.
The weakling king, her shuddering, nerveless tool,
   Would fain her act rebuke ;
But vain his trumpet-call when priestly rule
   Holds sceptre down with crook ;
When sword and pike are sanctified before
   The massacre for creed,
And demons, dripping with their victims' gore,
   Seek blessings on their deed.
              Boom ! boom !
              Swells through the gloom !

" Kill ! kill !" sounds hoarsely through the day and night.
   Can Providence be *here ?*

Yes HERE! Some lie concealed; some 'scape by flight,
    Swift-winged by mortal fear;
The father, burthened with his bleeding son,
    The hell-hounds at his heel,
Finds safety in a ready English gun,
    A stout boat's English keel;
The swooning maid, her lover's blood may stain,
    Seems one already sped;
Children crouch living 'neath the weltering slain,
    Saved by the very dead.
                    Boom! boom!
                    Still tolls for doom!

The grateful peasant screens the nobly born
    In coarsest rustic dress,
And sets him, reaping 'mong the standing corn,
    Some past kind act to bless;
Mothers claim others' infants as their own,
    Maternal instinct rife;
And till God's judgment day will ne'er be known,
    How love saves life with life!
Still—France one bleeding wound—each tainted gale
    Sobs out the tocsin knell,
From north to south one universal wail
    Echoes the fatal bell.
                    Boom! boom!
                    Death's note of doom!

"EN TOUTO NIKA!"

E read on the historic page
  The monarch Constantine,
  Whilst marching 'gainst a pagan foe,
 Invoked the Power divine
In choice of a religious creed
 To lead his steps aright,
To grant him knowledge of the truth,
 And aid him in the fight :—
When—in the dusky evening sky
 Appeared the Christian's sign,
The Cross—in glowing, dazzling light,
 Whence rayed the lustrous line,
    " In *this* overcome !"

The startled monarch stood amazed,
 Owned the God-given guide,
Upreared the standard of the Cross
 And fought—faith-fortified.

For, trusting not in human strength,
  He sought help from on high,
And ever in the cause of truth
  Marched but to victory.
Still far and wide his conquests spread,
  In temple, council, field,
And wheresoe'er the Cross was reared,
  And God in Christ revealed,
          In *this* overcame !

And so the Christian, whensoe'er
  Assailed by doubts or fears,
Should turn the inner eye above
  And lo ! the Cross appears !
A promise to the fainting heart,
  A guide in doubts thick shade,
A refuge to the penitent
  In cheering light arrayed.
Or, should his soul be. e'er assailed
  By foes without, within,
Raise but the standard of the Cross
  And quell the hosts of sin ;
          In *this* overcome.

THE FOUNTAIN OF YOUTH.

In the decline of life, Juan Ponce De Leon, the sometime companion of Columbus, threw up in disgust his governorship of Porto-Rico; and having heard from some of the native Caribs that, in a land to the north-west, there was a spring which gave *perpetual youth* to all who bathed therein, he induced a few other adventurers to join him, and fitting up a small fleet, set sail in search of the miraculous fountain. The result was the discovery of Florida, long supposed to be an island. Sailing up the river St. John, the seamen named the place "Florida!" by involuntary acclamation. It was a wilderness of flowers. He was one of the early voyagers in search of El Dorado.

UAN Ponce De Leon has sailed away
 To a mythic isle in the farther west ;
 Has followed the sun for many a day,
Tracking it home to its burning nest.
He seeks not *now*, for the glory of Spain,
The land which runs golden in every vein ;
He's braving the hungry, treacherous main,
With a craving stronger than greed of gain,—
 Has the Fountain of Youth in quest.

Count not the years since he stood on a deck
 By the side of Columbus, with eyes of fire,

And a brain too ardent to dream of wreck,
  Whilst a New World waited their wild desire ;
Count not the years he has governed, at ease,
That teeming isle in the tropic seas,
Ere he quarrelled with Spain and her grandees,
And once more shook out his sails to the breeze,
  In a spirit that could not tire.

Like snow on the fiery volcano's crest
  . Is the silvery glint in his ebon hair ;
As the plough's deep furrows on earth's brown breast
  Are the lines his forehead begins to wear :
And never a missal from monkish pen
Was more clearly written for learnèd ken
Than those lines proclaiming that men are *men ;*   •
But Leon has answered his own heart's " When ? "
  With a shout that has rent the air.

" It is not for manhood to sit and wait
  The advancing foe with impassive hands.
Shall age come on boldly and storm the gate
  Of Leon, the victor of seas and lands ?
Nay—while my pulses yet quicken and beat
To the dancing step of feminine feet,
And while red lips quiver my lips to meet,
And every sense has a joy to greet,
  Is the time to arrest life's sands !

"Shall the bright Fount of Perpetual Youth,
　　Circled by rainbows, flash out in the sun,
And Ponce De Leon be idle forsooth,
　　Its marvellous waters unsought for, unwon?
Spaniards, be ours the adventurous quest
Of the radiant Isle, and Fountain blest,
And ours to bring home from the golden West,
That treasure no mortal has yet possessed,
　　Fit to quench e'en an angel's drouth !"

Dauntless, and sanguine their youth to renew,
　　They have sunwards sailed o'er an unknown sea,
With hearts that need to be fearless and true,
　　To fight with the waves and weed on their lee.
On, through the silence and dark of the night ;
On, through the silence and glare of the light ;
Baffled by calm, or by storm in its might ;
Weary, discouraged, no haven in sight ;—
　　" Ha !　Whate'er can that perfume be ?"

A faint, sweet breath seems to come on the breeze,
　　The mingled essence of odorous things,
With soft suggestions of blossoms and trees,
　　And tropical birds with gorgeous wings.
And lo ! there *are* birds in the fervid sky ;
Lo ! land is discerned by De Leon's eye :

" Land ! land !" is each seaman's ecstatic cry,
Reprieved from the death he had feared to die,
    Afar from Youth's magical springs.

" Florida !   Florida !   Fair land of Flowers !"
Flies like an echo from ship unto ship.
" Florida !" answer gay birds from their bowers,
    Catching the word from humanity's lip ;
Flushing the face of De Leon with pride,
As up the opaline river they glide,
Carried along by the inflowing tide,
Gazing enamoured, as one on a bride ·
    Whom he fears from his clasp may slip.

" Thanks be for aye to the holy St. John,
    This is an Eden of beauty and bliss !
Every aroma the zephyrs waft on,
    Tells of some nectar the honey-bees kiss ;
Vines clasp the trees, and the trees woo the vine ;
Palm and banana wave o'er the rich pine ;
Grandly the sun sets, but scarce less divine,
The effluent tints of bird, insect and bine,
    Where blooms burn with glory like his.

" Here ends our toil ! for Youth's fountain must be
    Shrined in this verdurous isle of delight ;
Life, glowing life is in all that we see ;
    Stars are alive in the forest at night !

Cut we a path through the blossoming bowers.
Soon will the water delicious be ours ! "
Parrot and mocking-bird echo for hours,
" Fountain of Youth in this island of flowers ! "
  In most exquisite irony.

Under the sycamores, out on the hill,
  Fountain and rivulet ripple and run ;
Youth's living fount is a mystery still ;
  And the search ends—as the seekers begun.
Parrot and mocking-bird chant their refrain
Long after Leon re-crosses the main,
Proud of the wreath he has given to Spain ;
Long after death seals the fount in his brain,
  And the Fount Immortal *is* won !

PENT IN THE CITY.

BRICK and mortar hem me in !
    I, who love the fields and trees,
    Hear but the ceaseless din
Of traffic, toil, and sin,
    Not the murmur of the brooklet and the breeze.

The swift seasons come and go ;
    Golden king-cups star the grass ;
June's crimson roses blow ;
Rich dahlias are aglow,
    And the holly hangs o'er pools that are like glass :

But the same dull round is mine,
    In the same cramped blank of wall.
I know the sun does shine,
And feel his rays divine,
    But the very sun seems cumbered with a pall.

Sparrows twitter in the eaves,
  (I've no lark within a cage),
But blackbird bowered in leaves,
Nor linnet from the sheaves,
  Nor glad nightingale my thirst for song assuage.

There are woodland haunts I knew
  When my life was young and sweet,
When hours were all too few,
And skies were always blue,
  As the harebell and the speedwell at my feet.

But those woods are far away,
  If we count the years as miles ;
My hair has changed to gray,—
My heart well-nigh to clay,
  Since I, wild-flower laden, sat on sylvan stiles.

And these never-ending streets,—
  Wherein now my lot is cast,
Where every pulse that beats
The same sad song repeats,
  That human life is hurrying on too fast,—

Seem to close and crush me in ;
  Not a gap left for escape
From their oppressive din
To heath or crystal linn,
  Yellow sea-beat sands, or breezy headland cape.

I am tied to city ways ;
   I am bound as to a wheel ;
But at my will I raise
The ghosts of former days,
   And from the present to the past I steal.

Then the close walls fade and melt,
   Grass and ferns spring at my feet,
Trees circle as a belt,
Beech-mast and acorns pelt,
   And the perfume of the woods comes passing sweet.

And I linger in the lanes,
   Plaiting rushes as I go,
And list the birdie's strains,
And joy runs through my veins,
   Such pure joy as youth and summer only know.

And some pleasant cheery face,
   Some lithe and supple form,
Imparts a crowning grace,
To sun the shady place,
   And to quicken up the pulses fresh and warm.

Therefore, I may thank my God,
   That, although in city pent,
My childhood's footsteps trod
Greenwood and daisied sod,
   And memory wields a wand that should content :

For within this selfsame town
    Exist some hapless men,
Whose sun of life goes down
As it rose, 'mid tear and frown,
    With no summer field or forest in their ken.

CRAZY KATE.

EVER she wanders along the shore,
　　Alike in the glow and shine,
　　Alike when the awful waters roar,
And sprinkle her with their brine ;
Watching each tiny speck of a sail
　　As men look out for a star ;
Wistful eyes and monotonous wail
　　Asking the distance afar,
" When will he come back o'er the sea ?
When, oh, when will our meeting be ? "

Her hair was brown, and her young eye clear,
　　Her raiment was neat and trim,
When the first faint shadowings of fear
　　Brought her here to look for him,
When the crested waves ran swift and high,
　　And their white foam lipped her feet,

And thunder-peals from an angry sky
  Were rocking her boulder-seat,
As she cried for him across the sea,
" When, oh, when will our meeting be ? "

Her locks are grey and her eye is dim,
  Her dress is as worn as she,
Yet still she looks and watches for him
  To come back over the sea :
Heeding no winds that flutter her rags,
  No sun that scorches her brow ;
Pacing the sands, or climbing the crags,
  Peering for pennant and prow ;
Ever that wail is sent o'er the sea,
" When, oh, when will our meeting be ? "

The very sea-birds skimming the wave,
  Hearing the piteous cry,
Have borne its echoes unto a grave
  That lies 'neath an Arctic sky ;
Yet answer none have they brought again,
  In all of the thirty years
She has watched with crazy heart and brain,
  And eyes that have burnt up tears.
But soon *she* will sail for the crystal sea,
And *then*, oh, *then* will their meeting be !

THE LOVERS' HOUR.

HEN the evening sun goes down,
 And the daisies close their eyes;
Ere dusk wrinkles to a frown,
Or the stars blink in the skies;
When the dew and zephyrs light
 Woo the perfume from the flower,
When the day is meeting night
 Is the lovers' hour.

Gloaming is the trysting time:
 Hardest outlines soften then;
Common mortals grow sublime;
 Love and twilight soften men.
Feelings hidden from the light
 Shrink not to assert their power;
And when day is wooing night,
 Is the lovers' hour.

Twilight veils with kindly grace
    Blushes burning on the cheek,
When the timid upturned face
    Coyly answers eyes that speak ;
Lip meets lip, its troth to plight ;
    Rapture keen is love's sweet dower ;
Then, when day is kissing night,
    Is the lover's hour.

THE MINSTREL'S MEED.

MINSTREL lifted his voice on high :—
 Full in the ears of the gathering throng,
 A pean of war and victory,
Like the blast of a trumpet, rolled along ;
And fierce and fast did the pulses beat,
 To the time and tune of that martial strain,
Of every man in the crowded street ;—
 But a woman wept,—she thought of the slain.

Anon did the minstrel change his theme,—
 Again did the pulses of men leap high :
Wine ran red through his song like a stream,
 Flashed in his cheek, and gave fire to his eye.
" Ho, for the vintage ! " he trolled and sang,
 " Ho, for the vintage ! "—but as the refrain
With bacchant shout through the welkin rang,
 Sad tears from a woman fell down like rain.

Soft and low as the breath of the breeze,
  Pensive and tender as coo of the dove,
Strong as billows of resonant seas,
  Warmly impassioned, he warbled of love—
Love, its ecstasy, ardour, and bliss ;
  Love that ran thrilling through bosom and brain ;
And manhood listened and longed to kiss,
  But a woman wept,—she had felt its pain.

Once more did the minstrel change his note,
  To the gifts of mind and their meed of fame ;
And song poured forth from his swelling throat
  With a sense of power in its words of flame.
He sang of song that should never die,
  And of thoughts to outlive the speeding years ;
And men responded with cheer and cry,—
  A woman answered alone with tears.

With every change of his changing song
  Had the hearts of his hearers throbbed and beat,
But not a tribute from all that throng
  As the tears of the woman came so sweet.
All that sets passions of men aglow
  Must have its under-current of pain,
So the minstrel felt that *his* fame would grow,
  Warmed by that sunshine and fed by that rain.

FALLING LEAVES.

HE wind its trump hath blown
    Adown the dell,
  And lo ! what leaves are strown
On yon grey stone,
And o'er the well !

Like human hopes they fall—
    Hopes born in Spring,
  When Nature's cuckoo-call
    Wakes life in all,
    And everything.

Leaves matron Summer nurst
    On sunny slopes,
  Where their young verdure first
    To beauty burst ;—
    Leafage and hopes.

But the autumnal gust
　　That sweeps life's dell,
Blows leaves as red as rust
　　Into the dust,
　　And death's dark well.

HAUNTED!

AND so, it is said, you are haunted !
    My friend, we are haunted all ;
    And every homestead holds a ghost
That ever has held a pall.

Do you think that the empty cradle
    Has never a ghost within ?
Or the unused nursery table
    Hears never a ghostly din ?

Think you there is never a patter
    Of unseen feet on the floor ?
Or that never a voiceless clamour
    Floats in through the garden door ?

Is there ever a maid or widow
    Whose love lies under a stone,
Who holds not a ghost to her aching heart,
    To cherish and call her own ?

Is there ever a grey-haired beauty
Looks not in her glass to see—
No time-worn face—but the phantom form
Of the belle she was wont to be?

Was there ever a wretch abandoned,
A waif from the hour of birth,
Whose unknown mother was not to him
A ghost on the dreary earth?

Could there ever be man or woman,
Pacing through lane or street,
Who could not extend an open hand
Some shadowy friend to greet?

Could there ever be man or woman
So lonely and loveless through life,
Was never haunted by kith or kin,
Spirit of peace or strife?

Could there ever be human being
With heart so narrow and small
That never a ghost could hide therein,
To waken at Memory's call?

There are some with vision beclouded
Who see not all that they might;
And some, of a finer essence born,
Who see with the inner sight.

To these the past hath its phantoms,
  More real than solid earth ;
And to these death does not mean decay,
  But only another birth.

A FOREST FANCY.

HAREBELLS and fern from a forest nook !
  Oh ! leave them with me and let me dream !—
I see them growing beside a brook,
And hear the wimpling wash of the stream.

I watch from a round red knob uprise,
  Crosier-headed, the feathery fronds,
Till graceful plumes under summer skies
  Wave, as rejoicing o'er broken bonds ;

And close by the green umbrageous fern,
  Which arches over a fairy bower,
A pendulous blue inverted urn
  Where goblins shelter from sun and shower,—

Whence music, audible unto them,
  Floats on the air, as, by zephyrs rung,
The harebell, on its delicate stem
  So daintily poised, is lightly swung.

The fiery sun goes down to his bath,
  Moon-bright lances are shot through the trees,
Wee elves come trooping by many a path
  As harebell chimes swell out on the breeze.

The cricket answers with shrill delight
  That harebell summons still ringing out,
As glowworm lamps are lit for the night
  And echo thrills with a fairy shout.

For, guarded by sprites, with spears of grass,
  To mossy dais and acorn throne,
The elfin queen and her courtiers pass
  To the palace of fern she calls her own.

In feast and frolic they while the time
  With feats too deft for a form of clay ;
Or dance to the pensile harebell's chime ;—
  Dawn breaks—the fairies are fled away !

With daylight cometh a fair young maid,
  Her touch as light as an elf's might be,
Beguiles the harebell and fern from the glade,
  And brings the forest and fays to me.

THE OLD FOOT-BRIDGE.

N the old rustic foot-bridge met Alice and he,
   On the frail wooden foot-bridge away from the
   town,
As a bird sang its vespers above in a tree,
   And the sun in its splendour was journeying down.
They had parted years past in the strength of disdain,
And they met, face to face, in love's weakness again,
With a start, and a throb—not of pleasure, but pain.

Was the flush on her cheek from the crimsoning west?
   Was it twilight that deepened the shade on his brow?
Was that cry from the bird just alit on its nest,
   Or the gasp of a heart which repented a vow?
Nay, with song-notes alone the broad chestnut leaves stirred;
And too human the anguish that broke without word
In the cry which was smothered ere palpably heard.

What had drawn the twain thither that glorious eve,
  To a spot so replete with the keenest of woe?
Were there tears to be shed the full heart to relieve,
  Where pride had dealt each so relentless a blow?
Or came Alice to muse on the past—as the past;
Or came Herbert to rave o'er the die he had cast,
That they met without warning, and *there* too,—at last?

That foot-bridge, where first, in the newness of bliss,
  She had looked in the stream as he looked in her eyes,
Where her lips learned to answer his passionate kiss,
  And his arm clasped her fast as an exquisite prize:
Could that rotten old plank have outlasted their truth?
Could the rail they had leaned on in confident youth
Still exist, when affection's bonds snapped without ruth?

" Ay, birds sing, and trees bloom, though hearts wither and
    fade;
  And the sun warms the earth though man's bosom be chill;
So the crazy old foot-bridge has not been remade,
  And, more lasting than love, the hand-rail is there still;
More enduring than ours "— " Ah!" Eyes meet, lips turn
    pale—
Alice grasps for support at the outstretching rail,—
Even *that*, as she trusts it, proves faithless and frail.

Hark! another cry startles the birds from their nest,
  As the waters close over that pang of surprise.

'Tis the anguish of manhood rent out of a breast
  Barred and steeled against love by the foulest of lies !
Then—a crash, and a plunge in the eddying stream,
The past all forgotten—the present a dream ;—
Love had leaped back to life with that half-suppressed scream.

There's a race with the river, so cruel and swift ;
  A fierce fight, with the strength of remorseful despair :
It is more than a life that is floating adrift ;—
  He must save her or perish ! He clutches her hair,
The bright curls so caressingly fondled of yore.
Joy ! he holds her, his Alice, he draws her ashore.—
Oh ! has fate but united, to sunder once more ?

Nay, the love that has fought for her life with the wave
  Will fight for her, ay, with the Angel of Death ;
And those passionate prayers must be potent to save,
  For the livid lips warm with perceptible breath.
Resentment, estrangement, like nightmares are gone :—
Only love could so cling to the breast she leans on :
They are linked for the future—two beings in one.

CRAVING REST.

H ! for the leisure to lie and to dream
By some woodland well, or some rippling
stream,
With a cool green covert of trees overhead,
And fern or moss for my verdurous bed ;

To rest, and to trifle with rushes and reeds,
Threading wild berries like chaplets of beads,
Letting the breeze fan my feverish brows,
Listening the birds sing their summery vows.

Oh ! for the leisure to lie without thought,
Upon the mind's anvil the ingot unwrought ;
The hammers that beat in my temples at rest ;
Calm in life's atmosphere, calm in the breast.

To loll or to saunter, to laugh or to weep,
Awaken the echoes, or silence to keep,
With no human being at hand to intrude,
Or ! question the wherefore of manner or mood.

Oh ! for such leisure to rest, and to stray
In green haunts of nature, if but for a day ;
Through leaves to look up at the sky from the sod,
Alone with my heart, my griefs, and my God !

LIFE'S SONG AND SUNSHINE.

WHY blame me that my songs are sad ?
    If ye would have them gay,
    Restore me that which made me glad,
Life's sunshine and its May.
True, cloudlets flecked the rays divine,
    Thorns hid beneath the bloom ;
But then, intoxicant as wine
    Were radiance and perfume.
And through the clust'ring pink and white,
    What recked I of the thorn,
While tint and fragrance brought delight,
    And hope was newly born ?
But, crimson-tipped, or creamy white,
    Each petal was a wing ;
And, ah ! the flowers alone took flight,
    The thorns remained to sting.

If ye would have a joyous strain,
  Bring back my youthful lyre,
Still every pulse that throbs with pain,
  Renew life's fading fire ;
Bring round me once the loving hands
  That clasped in mine of old;
Open mine ears to seraph bands
  Touching their harps of gold ;
And give warm love my love to bless,
  Kind thoughts for kindly deeds ;
Bring tenderness and gentleness
  To staunch the heart that bleeds ;
Obliterate the memories
  Of cruel wrong and scorn,
If ye would have such melodies
  As joy sings in its morn.

THE BLACKBIRD'S NEST.

HERE'S a narrow fringe of coppice by the borders
   of the brook
   That skirts the open field-path to our ancient house
of prayer ;
And I know that midst the brambles, if I felt inclined to
look,
I should find a blackbird's nest, for I'm sure that it is there.

I know that I could find it, with its eggs of blue and brown,
In a lowly net of branches, hid from schoolboys' prying eyes,
A few paces from the alder on the side the nearest town ;
But I dare not show you where, lest you make his nest a
prize.

He has oft tried to mislead me, and flitting far away,
From a thicket in the distance has tuned his mellow throat;
But I mostly find him seated on an overhanging spray,
Where his mate within the nest can give an answering note.

When the sun shines hot and fierce he sits moody in the
    glare,
But when genial showers are falling he plays his wondrous
    pipe,
And he joins the village anthem as it floats upon the air,
And I sometimes think he asks when the cherries will be ripe.

For he dearly loveth cherries—but the surly-hearted clod
Who has no ear for melody beyond the chink of gain,
Will begrudge the summer payment of this worker, sent by
    God
To free the springtide growth from the pests on fruit and
    grain.

He may shoot the thrush and blackbird, for they only come
    in pairs ;
He may spoil the warblers' nests, thread their eggs upon a
    string ;
But when insects come in myriads to defeat his sanguine
    cares,
He will wish he'd spared the blackbird, and his nest, in early
    spring.

ERE THE NIGHT.

I LOOK out across the waters
    To the gold and crimson west,
    Where the regal sun is drawing
Evening's veil before his breast ;
Ere, with kindly care for mortals
    Who are weary and o'erworn,
He permits night's dusky portals
    To close o'er him until morn ;
And I gaze upon his glory
    Till I feel no more forlorn.

I had been o'ertried and driven
    Ere I brought my boat to shore,
For the wind had been untoward,
    And the current mocked my oar ;
But the baffling breeze tore past me,
    Cheering zephyrs glassed the tide,
And ere evening's shades o'ercast me
    I have touched the hither side,
And in yonder sunset glory
    I see hope retypified.

THE MOUNTAIN STREAM.

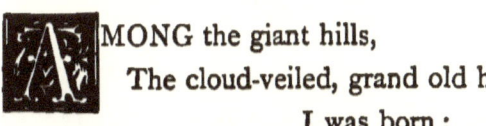MONG the giant hills,
    The cloud-veiled, grand old hills,
              I was born ;
And the mist with tiny rills
Softly fed me night and morn.

The spirits of the snow,
The soft delicious snow,
            O'er my head
Shook their pinions to and fro,
Till their plumage filled my bed.

I grew, as grows a child,
A laughing, lisping child
            At the breast ;
And my mountain-mother smiled
As my granite lips caressed.

No drop of rain or dew,
Of pure pellucid dew,
           Could I drink ;
But I swelled with life anew,
And too narrow was my brink.

Then, as a restless boy,
A brawling, wayward boy,
           Out of bounds,
On I leapt with noisy joy,
Fleet as stag outstripping hounds,

Headlong, o'er stone and rock,
O'er rough and craggy rock,
           Plunging deep,
Till I staggered with the shock
And in spray was forced to weep.

Then, mad, and stung with shame,
Hiding in glens for shame,
           Sullen, dark,
Till I flashed to light again,
Fresh and gleeful as a lark.

'Mid pealing heather-bells,
Sweet, chiming, purple bells,
           Did I mate ;
And my wedded bosom swells
As I onward roll elate.

Now see me in my prime,
My full developed prime, ·
                    Sweep along ;
Though monotonous as time,
Yet sonorous as song :

A noble mountain stream,
A torrent of a stream,
                    Giving back
From my sheen the sunset beam,
And the silvery flying rack.

The solitary hills,
My old ancestral hills,
                    Sigh for me ;
Yet though every ripple thrills
With fondest memory,

My stream will see its nest,
Its hoary mountain nest,
                    Nevermore ;
For ambition fills my breast,
And I seek a wider shore.

I quit the shade of pines,
Dark, moaning, perfumed pines,
                    Fleet and fast ;
Through the world my course inclines,
And I seek the sea at last.

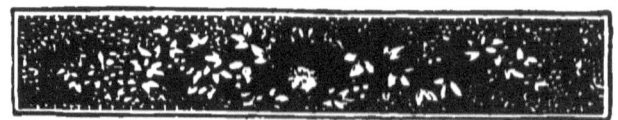

LET THEM SLEEP.

HERE'S a twitter from the poplars,
    And a flutter in the limes,
        For the dawn is slowly breaking,
And the birdies wake betimes ;
But the trees still cast a shadow
    On the mill beside the stream,
Where the unawakened inmates
    In serenest slumber dream,
As though the wash of waters
    Was a lullaby supreme.

But the dawn is creeping upwards,
    And the birds their matins trill,
To awake the drowsy sleepers
    In the cottage and the mill ;
But the human, worn with labour,
    Has the longer need of rest,

And while Night still spreads her pinions
   (Like a blessing from the blest)
Let them sleep, to wake as blithely
   As the birdlings in the nest.

There be those among the song-birds
   Of the dense and stifling town
To whom the night brings no repose,
   And the dawn comes with a frown,
Who would gladly sink to slumber
   Like the miller and the thrush,
And awaken fresh and buoyant
   When the dawn comes with a blush
But *their* nests are not mid lindens,
   And their stream runs with a rush.

THE CHURCH OF THE PILGRIM FATHERS.

O the green primeval forests across the western wave,
Oppression drove a slender band of true hearts strong and brave :
They could not think as others thought, nor feel as others felt,
Nor obey the royal edict to kneel where others knelt ;
But they had heard of shores afar by priestly feet untrod ;
So they sought that land for conscience' sake—their guiding star, their God.

No gallant bark was theirs to steer, only a time-worn boat,
With stores as small as seamanship, and yet she kept afloat,
For Faith and Hope were at the helm amid the tempest's roar ;
But Hope was dead, and Faith was numb, before they reached the shore,
Where children faint, and women pale, first pressed their feeble feet,
And stretched out hungry hands to clasp their last few grains of wheat.

Five grains of wheat!—ay, think of it!—were all for each
    thin hand,
When the *Mayflower* had sailed her last, and brought her
    freight to land;
Yet—for, prayer and praise unfettered, at once the welkin
    rang
With the anthems of thanksgiving those grateful pilgrims
    sang,
Ere a roof was theirs to shelter, or fruit their parched lips
    prest—
They had touched the land of promise, and left to God the
    rest!

And they, who from cathedral aisles had fled in fear and
    scorn,
In a grander, God-built temple, could worship eve and morn;
Beneath the interlacing boughs, like arches overhead,
Where verdure of a virgin turf a silent carpet spread,
And stately as a pillared shaft uprose each tall tree-bole,
With the sun-rays—God's bright fingers—to glorify the
    whole.

CHALLENGED.

Y trusty rapier, shall I meet
  This common brawler of the street?
  Or fling his challenge in his teeth,
An honest soldier's arm beneath?
  There is no tarnish on thy blade,
    No spot upon thy name;
  No man can say I am afraid,
    No man belie my fame.

Ne'er have I drawn thee in a cause
Opposed to honour, truth, or laws;
Ne'er have I drawn thee on a foe,
Lacking good reason for the blow :—
  A woman wronged, a comrade pressed,
    A rogue to put to flight;
  But never was thy point addressed
    Unto a baser fight.

Ne'er did I draw thee on a friend ;
Ne'er urged a stripling to his end ;
Ne'er thrust my sword in tavern fray ;
Ne'er picked a quarrel by the way.
 Oft has my temper, like thy steel,
  Been sharply touched and tried ;
 But men must think as well as feel,
 And turn hot wrath aside.

Yet we wear swords for use, not show ;
And thou hast served me well, I trow,
Hast helped mine arm to save my head,
Or I had lain among the dead :
 For men, of whatsoe'er degree,
  Make foes as well as friends ;
 And proud the athlete well may be
 Whom such a blade defends.

And hold I it a sacred trust,
As I would keep thee free from rust,
To see thy surface has no stain
Of blood which brings the curse of Cain :
 And better let this braggart boast
  Among his ruffian brood,
 Than let thy blade with his be crost,
 Ensanguined with his blood.

I hold not honour on his breath,
Nor holds he power of life or death.
I who have fought in tented field,
And never yet was known to yield,—
    I, who know every trick of fence,
      Supple of wrist and limb,—
    To meet, on whatsoe'er pretence,
      Would be to murder him !

To God, to country, and to throne,
I owe the life I call mine own ;
And duty bids me guard that life
From lawless feud, assassin's knife ;
    It may be, by my trusty steel,
      But not in dual fight :
    New wounds can not an old one heal,
      No wrong can make a right.

I will *not* meet the senseless wight
Who sent his challenge overnight ;
Mine shall not be the crime and shame
Of murder with another name.
    And *so*, my shining blade, I'll keep
      My honour free from stain ;
    No mother for her son shall weep,
      By me in duel slain.

I

BRIDAL ROBES.

A BRIDAL robe should be
　　A dress to be worn for the day,
　　Then laid aside with all perfumes rare,
A treasure to guard with lifelong care,
　　A relic for ever and aye.

And never meaner use
　　Should sully its delicate snow;
The bride's last robe in her maidenhood
Should be kept as perfect, pure, and good,
　　As when first it was donned, I trow.

For ever a dainty type
　　Of her chastity pure and white,
Folded up, like a rose in the bud,
Its beauty unseen, but understood
　　By all who can think aright.

Text from the marriage morn,
In its silence to preach through life,
Of duties, put on with every fold,
To change that life's silver into gold,
If love link true husband and wife.

And not till Death should call
The tried wife to *his* bridal bed
Should that well-saved robe again be worn, ·
Or that orange wreath again adorn
The auburn or lint-white head ;

And only wife who kept
As spotless her life as her dress,
Be honoured to wear her bridal gown,
Be honoured to wear her bridal crown,
When Death shall her pale lips press.

THE COST OF COAL.

WHAT! gone !—is he really gone?
　　Shall I never behold him more?
　　Ne'er hear again his manly tread
　On the bricks of our cottage floor;
Or his blithe whistle, so sharp and clear,
The bairnies would clap their hands to hear?

Gone! It's like a dreadful dream!
　He was here scarce an hour ago;
And now you say our Tom lies dead
　In the depths of the pit below!
I cannot credit the tidings sore,
I cannot think we shall meet no more!

Oh, Nancy, lass! well may you weep
　For the brother you've lost to-day!
Tears should *my* burning eyeballs steep,
　But my heart seems turned to clay:
My very brain is numb as a stone,—
Can our Tom be killed, and we alone?

Oh, Nance ! if but my tears would flow,
   They might wash the ache from my heart ;
But only wives so widowed know
   What it is to love and to part ;
To feel that the husband, cold and dead,
Had paid with his life for our daily bread !

" Killed, as the cage went down the shaft,
   Through the snap of a faulty chain ! "
Oh, God ! how it comes crashing down
   On the top of my own poor brain !
And every sense seems to reel and swim,
To think of a world which holds not him !

This morn, as he went off to work,
   He kissed both of his bairns and me ;
Ah ! little then thought he or I
   Of the parting that it would be !
As little his bairnies seem to care,
Or *know* of their loss and my despair.

Dead ! deep down in the darksome pit,
   A wreck to be shut from my sight !
Ah ! what think folk in cheerful homes
   Of the cost of their fire and light ?
Yet thankful the wives of men may be
Who work above ground in security.

THE PEARL OF PEARLS.

ELICATE, pure, and pale as a pearl
Was Clara, my sister's orphan girl;
A dying charge to a brother's care,
A gem to guard as a treasure rare,
A sensitive, shy, and blushful thing,
Too young to set in a golden ring—
   So fair was she.

And I had a son who was all to me,
Though he had flaws which I could not see;
And under his college cap and gown
Sprang germs of vice which ran wild in town.
But I shut my eyes on cards and dice,
And far too easy was my advice
   For such as he.

He cast his eyes on our pearl of pearls,
Saw glinting gold in her auburn curls,
And he bent his head, and bowed his knee,
As unto a shrined divinity.

He wrung her heart with his sighs and tears;
She wept, but answered, through months and years,
    "It cannot be."

Then he turned to me to bend her will:
Her sad-voiced "nay" was decisive still;
And never a word said she to me
Wherefore she dreaded his wife to be;
So I cast the clinging girl adrift,
And held back the fruits of her father's thrift
    Most knavishly.

I shut my ears to the cry of "Shame!"
And left the land with my tainted name;
But Clara's coin burnt holes in my purse;
My thankless son knew alone to curse;
Till round my head, as a tempest swirls,
A voice that asked for her pearl of pearls
    Came haunting me.

I was old, and worn, and had lost a limb—
Lost in vain efforts to rescue him,—
Driven by conscience back to a land
Where never a friend would take my hand;
Snow on my heart, and snow on my head,
Snow on the pavement beneath my tread,
    Chilled frostily.

Warm hands clasp mine in a quiet square,
A stranger's hat is raised from his hair :
" Dear uncle ! my husband ! Here we live ! "
Had she forgotten ? could she forgive ?—
Here, on their hearth, among Clara's girls,
I learn why she is a pearl of pearls,—
She forgave ME !

THE NEW CHURCH.

NOTHER temple to the Lord !
Another house of prayer,
Where two or three may gather
To find *Him* present there :
Where two or three devout ones
May meet to pray and praise,
And bide the "still small whisper"
That follows Horeb's blaze.

Where some *one* reckless scoffer,
Some *one* with dull deaf ears,
May hear God's awful thunder
When Sinai's crest uprears :
Some *one* appalled by Moses
Stern on his mount of flame,
May Jesus hear, from Olivet,
The "law of love" proclaim.

Where one or more despairing,
  Soul-weary and oppressed,
May cast their sins on Calvary,
  And find eternal rest:
Where 'mong the light and thoughtless
  Of fashion's giddy train,
Some scattered seeds may germinate
  And flourish—not in vain.

Where the ireful and contentious
  May grow ashamed of strife,
And the sacred code of morals
  May reform some vicious life:
Where the triple Christian graces
  Stand within the open door
To salute, with smiling faces,
  Alike the rich and poor.

What though amidst the many
  Drawn thither week by week
Few kneel in pious worship,
  Few come the Lord to seek:
If but two or three believers
  Are there to hear the Word,
CHRIST will be there to sanctify
  The Temple of the Lord.

Then build in hope, and build in faith
  The church of brick and stone,
Where souls shall learn the living way
  Unto the pure white throne :
By ones, by twos, through lapsing years,
  To cross the jasper sea ;
A countless host, whose sum is lost
  In God's infinity.

THE DAY OF REST.

OH, Sabbath, blessed day ! Oh, day of rest !
   Shade in life's burning noon ;
     Heavy and weary, care and toil opprest,
  I hail thee as a boon !
I long to lay the six days' burden down,
  Relax the cramping hand,
Ease the brain-tension, change the anxious frown,
  For smiles composed and bland.

I fain would set aside with work-day things
  All work-day thoughts and cares,
As though an angel came on shining wings
  To part life's wheat from tares.
I fain would send my aspirations far
  Beyond this grovelling clay,
Beyond the farthest ray of sun or star
  To Him who made the day.

I fain would travel somewhat on the track
  All saints of old have trod,
With fewer worldly imps to drag me back
  From paths which lead to God.
Not that I long to set the day apart
  For stiff, ascetic gloom :
I would but clear the chambers of my heart
  To give love wider room ;

To hold sweet intercourse with God and kin
  As Christ was God and man,
And let a flood of friendliness come in
  The six days cannot span ;
To use the day as not abusing it ;
  To learn in wisdom's school
How love of God with love of man may fit
  With duty's line and rule.

Oh, Sabbath ! day of quietude and peace,
  Like water, light, and air,
Thy blessings are around us and increase,
  We know not how or where.
Yet, oh ! too oft thy blessings men despise,
  Deny thy sacred birth ;
And only by thy loss can learn to prize
  Or feel the Sabbath's worth.

RETRIBUTION!

A GRAND and stately place,
  Built for a noble race,
  And held with courtly grace
When Bess was queen :
With battlemented wall,
A turret strong and tall,
And spacious banquet-hall
  With carven screen.

A mansion of the past ;
Ancestral, solid, vast,
Fitted to stand the blast
  Of war or time.
But, ah ! that ruin grim,
Looming through twilight dim,
'Mong trees no hand may trim,
  Succumbs to crime.

Yon eagle, cut in stone,
Sad, silent, and alone,

Could tell of strife and groan
Had he a tongue :
Could tell how cruel hate
Forced through that iron gate
The heir unto his fate,
In hideous wrong :

Could tell how yon green moat,
Where the usurper smote,
Opened again its throat
In after time :
How retribution there—
Mocking extremest care—
Drowned every son and heir
'Mid weeds and slime :

And how a sense of doom
Pervaded each old room ;
Till from the solemn gloom
The owners fled ;—
Fled ! gave the ancient pile,
Where none dared sing or smile,
To dust and all things vile,
In fear and dread.

UNTROD!

(FROM A PICTURE.)

HAT have we here?
Immensity, and power, and solitude.
The bristling crags spread out in rugged might.
The torrent rushes down, resistless, vast,—
Suggestive of illimitable lakes,
Or boundless plains of melting sun-kissed snow.
The grandest forest tree is here a dwarf
Beside that giant, hoar with froth and foam.
The clouds are big with thunder—no less voice
Could answer back the cataract's loud roar.
This is no home for puny things called men :
They would destroy its grandeur—utilize
That stream magnificent—quarry the crags—
Blot Nature's name from this her fairest page.
It is too great for man—'tis fit for God,—
And God alone dwells here.

WATCHERS BY THE SEA.

H, sparkling and clear in the setting sun
    Shone the dancing wavelets within the bay,
    As our fishing-boats sailed out, one by one,
To the depths where the gleaming mackerel lay ;
And we crowded the jetty, old and young,
    The weather-worn jetty that met the tide,
With gay good wishes on lip and tongue
    Of the widowed mother or blithe young bride ;
While we waved our kerchiefs with hearts at ease,
For the sun shone bright on the smiling seas ;
And fishermen's sweethearts, mothers, and wives,
Have hopeful hours in their anxious lives.

Yet midnight came with a thunderous shock ;
    Blue lightnings flashed o'er a turbulent bay ;
Mad breakers beat on the threatening rock,
    Drenching women and jetty with blinding spray.

The sky was as black as the boiling flood,
　Our faces as white as the frothy foam ;
But heedless of roar or of rain we stood,
　Waiting and watching—for love and for home.
Watching, with eyes that strained through the dark,
For sail or sign of a home-bound bark,
As fishermen's wives *must* watch and wait,
When tempests rave and the boats are late.

Oh, never did watchers so welcome the morn
　Under cold grey skies and pitiless rain,
As we anxious women, wet and forlorn,
　Still looking out o'er a billowy main.
And brighter than ever streak of the sun,
　Was the first white speck of a tattered sail ;
But we held our breath until one after one
　We counted our boats from the jetty rail.
Counted our boats—ah ! counted not *men !*—
Back my true love came never again.
Watch I, or wait, by the taunting tide,
Never comes Reuben back to his bride !

LAST WORDS ON DECK.

T is hard to part from thee, Nell,
　　Yet a sailor lives by the sea;
　　And every trip I take o'er the foam
But helps to keep all things taut at home,
　　For the old folk, Nell, and for thee.

The boat waits to bear thee back, Nell,
　　To perform thy part on the shore;
So, whilst I hold thee in my embrace,
Look up, my lass, with a cheerful face
　　And a promise to fret no more.

A sailor's wife should be brave, Nell,
　　Not tremble at every breeze;
For ne'er a wind that sweeps o'er the land
But cometh from that Almighty hand,
　　That holds in its hollow the seas.

Remember, the world is wide, Nell,
   And the storms that threaten our cot,
· Here raving in fierce terrific gales,
May come as breezes to fan our sails,
   Where the sun shines burning hot.

It will never do to droop, Nell;
   You must keep up the old folks' heart,
Sing a merry song, be fresh and gay;
Yet drop sometimes on your knees to pray
   For him who is leagues apart.

And be it comfort to thee, Nell,
   That wherever thy Tom may be,
Thy voice and thy smile will go with him,
Though farewell tears thy bright eye dim,—
   And he will be true to thee.

And now, good-bye; God bless thee, Nell!
   Capt'n calls, and I must obey.
One last fond kiss, for love and for hope;
And mind, whether handling sail or rope,
   Thy own Tom for his Nell will pray.

So, trust in Almighty God, Nell,
   Who alone can succour and save,
To bring o'er the perilous billows' foam,
Hearty and hale, to the folk at home,
   Thy sailor back over the wave.

A CHRISTMAS CAROL.

RING the bells out! far and wide
Send the echoes o'er the tide,
Telling to remotest earth
Death is vanquished, Hope has birth.

Ring the bells out! let them peal—
Christ is born our wounds to heal;
Christ is born, the Prince of Peace;
Lay down weapons, war should cease.

Ring the bells out! let them sound
Wheresoever guilt is found,—
Where are mourners by a grave;—
" Christ is born the lost to save."

Ring the bells out! let them bear
Christ's glad message through the air,
Every angry thought to still—
" Peace on earth, to man good-will."

Ring the bells out ! let them chase
Darkness from the saddest face ;
Life eternal—Light is born
With our Christ this joyous morn.

THANKSGIVING AT SEA.

"**H**URRAH !" the shout arose
    From sailors' hearts and lips,
    "We've vanquished England's foes—
Made matchwood of their ships !
From each volcanic gun
    Our red shot swept in showers;
Sails rent—masts fell—we won !
    The victory is ours !
In streams the red blood ran
    Upon our oaken deck,
Yet never flinched a man
    Till we fired on a wreck.
Now, masters of the sea,
    Our proud keel curbs the foam,
Hurrah ! for victory !
    For England, and for home !"

"Hush!"—Every lip is mute;
  There's silence on the sea;
In reverent salute
  Caps doff—bends every knee.
"My men, stout hearts and brave!
  Long have ye fought and well;
But God the victory gave—
  To *Him* let pæans swell."
At once a thousand raise,
  As from one vibrant throat,
A votive song of praise,
  Pealing with trumpet note—
"Praise to the Lord of Hosts,
  Omnipotent in might!
Praise to the uttermost;
  His arm defends the right!"

"Now, let us bend in prayer."—
  Well disciplined, they kneel
As though one heart throbbed there
  Within those frames of steel:
"O Ruler of the flood,
  Of nations, kings, and laws,
Absolve our souls from blood
  Shed in our country's cause.

Accept our thanks for life
  Spared to recross the main,
Spared for dear babe and wife
  We hope to clasp again."
"Amen!" rolls out afar;
  Then—to the sky's blue dome—
"Hurrah! hurrah! hurrah!
  For England, and for home!"

SPRINGTIME IN THE WOODS.

OME out, sweet wife, for a stroll in the woods,
 A stroll in the woods with me,
 To welcome spring with its bursting buds,
As the coy young leaves peep out of their hoods,
 And blush on the old beech tree.

We may look at the names I proudly cut
 Last spring on its willing bole,
And rest once again in the woodman's hut,
Where the first love-gift on your finger put,
 Held promise of soul to soul.

It is sweet, now a plainer circlet binds
 Our names and our lives in one,
To ramble again where the wood-path winds,
Retracing the growth of love in our minds,
 Spring sunshine leading us on ;—

Sweet to list to the ringdove's gentle coo,
    The trill of the linnet's throat,
To mark how the fluttering thrushes woo,
And listening, softly our vows renew,
    With as musical a note.

How the verdant freshness of young springtime
    Through our human tissue thrills,
Uplifting the common to the sublime,
With the force of a gifted minstrel's rhyme,
    Or sunset 'mong Alpine hills.

And here, in the woods, where the graceful ash
    Competes with the gnarlèd oak,
Whether sun shall burn or rain shall splash,
Whether runnels shall dry or rills shall dash,
    My being to rapture woke.

Let me stoop and gather this primrose pale
    (It grows where you dropped your glove),
With anemones, strong to brave the gale
When the blustering winds of March prevail,—
    Fair emblem of wedded love.

Spring promises ripen to autumn fruit,
    In trees, in loves, and in lives ;
But trees, loves, and lives alike bear the bruit
Of storms that threaten both blossom and root,
    Mellowing that which survives.

But fairer, farther, the promise of spring,
  Sunny and balmy and bright,
Sends our souls, dear wife, an uprising wing
To the promise of life, where angels sing,
  And no wintry wind can blight.

SAILING TOGETHER.

IN the sunlight, the glad sunlight,
  You and I, love, sailed together,
  When the waters mirrored clearly
Golden sky and purple heather;
And my oars beat back the wavelets
  To the tune you sang to me,
And the world was full of sunshine
  And of joy for you and me.

In the moonlight, life's pale moonlight,
  We are gliding o'er the lake,
Where the mountains cast their shadows
  Athwart our silvern wake;
But still my oars dip lightly
  To the low song sung to me,
And the moonbeams shimmer brightly
  On thy head, love, and on me.

THE BUGLE CALL.

HARK ! 'tis the bugle, the bugle of War !
 Banners are flying, and sabres unsheath ;
 Rifles and bayonets gleam from afar ;
Cannon drive lumbering over the heath ;
Bustle and stir from the east to the west ;
 Marching of troops from the north to the south ;
Spectacled grandams, and babes at the breast,
 Press for the last time the warrior's mouth ;
Wives from mute husbands are torn with a wrench ;
 Men steel their hearts 'mid the clangour of arms ;
Spades turn from tillage to dig and entrench,
 And beauty to glory surrenders its charms,
 At the blast of the bugle, the bugle of War !

Hark ! 'tis the bugle, the bugle of War !
 Sabres are clashing, and banners are rent ;
Rifles are cracking and blazing afar ;
 Skies to the cannon their thunders have lent.

There's neighing of chargers and trampling of hoofs,
  As they beat on the limbs and the faces of men ;
There's shrieking of women, and flaming of roofs,
  And crashing of trees that will ne'er rise again.
The God-given harvest beat down and accurst,
  Trod with the vintage of blood into mire ;
Pillage, and slaughter, and crime of the worst,
  Riot and rampant—all passions afire—
  At the bray of the bugle, the bugle of War !

Hark ! 'tis the bugle, the bugle of Peace !
  Sounds o'er the battle-field—over the slain,
Hushes the strife, bids artillery cease,
  Thrills through the dying stretched out on the plain.
Hark ! how the call rings o'er valley and hill !
  " Light bivouac fires—weary warriors, rest ! "
Up, tender-eyed Pity, to save, not to kill ;
  Go forth on thy errand, the blessing and blest !
Softly, white snow wreathes a shroud for the dead,
  A mantle to hide the red deed War has done ;
Stern foemen shake hands where their fellows have bled,
  And mercy can breathe—now the battle is done—
  In the note of the bugle, the bugle of Peace !

WHEN SHALL IT BE?

HEN shall it be, love? When shall it be?
I languish with waiting, dear. Nellie, for thee.
The birds have long mated in thicket and tree,
The ripe hay is mown upon upland and lea,
But my dear one still lingers in maidenhood free ;
And, what though shy promises answer each plea,
Hope and promises ripen no harvest for me :
Oh, Nellie, sweet Nellie, say when shall it be?

The snowdrops hung pale 'neath the frost-bitten moon
When I sought your love first, and you granted the boon
Now, the sun and the year have the fervour of noon,
Your cheeks take their tint from the roses of June ;
But I hang at your heels like a cowardly loon,
With the heart of a woman, to sicken and swoon
For the bliss that rounds life with its holiest rune :
Oh, Nellie, be mine, love, and let it be soon !

SNOW.

OT in the city, in the crowded street,
    Not 'mong the haunts of men,
    Where the ceaseless tramp of countless feet
  Would crush thee out again,
    Fall thou, fair snow.

Not on our grimy roofs and miry ways,
  Where soot-flakes rest and cling ;
Not through the vaporous fog, whose murky haze
  Would smirch a cherub's wing,
    Fall thou, pure snow.

Out on the mountain, on the upland moor,
  Over the fertile vale,
O'er park and woodland, hall, and cottage poor,
  Shake out thy pinions pale,
    Angel of snow.

L

Where country children greet thee with a shout,
   And catch thee in their play,
The fur-clad darling, and the ragged lout,
   Rejoicing on their way,
      Fall thou, fair snow.

Spread thy white mantle out o'er mother earth,
   Keep warm her naked breast ;
Broad fields will thank thee with prolific birth,
   And man through thee be blest,
      Thou guardian snow.

Give to the wintry woods a crowning grace,
   And from the spreading plain,
Look at the sky with pure unsullied face,
   Where is no fear of stain,
      Thou spotless snow.

But far from the loud city's crowded ways,
   Wing thy unwhispering flight ;
Soil not thy virgin whiteness in its maze—
   Mammon has no delight
      In falling snow.

Hush ! the soft snow is drifting to the ground
   In eloquent rebuke !
I seem to hear a sermon without sound,
   And listen as I look
      Where falls the snow.

Yes ! in the city, in the crowded street
   Among the haunts of men,
Though the rough tramp of countless busy feet
   May crush it out again,
      Should fall the snow.

In the dark alleys, in the stifling lanes,
   Preaching, without a creed,
It leaves a lesson on the broken panes,
   In language all may read—
      " Be pure as snow."

The matchless loveliness of every flake
   Informs the dullest eye :
Rough walls, coarse garbage, shapes of beauty take
   The poorest may descry,
      Where falls the snow.

The gutter children hail thee with a shout,
   Thou cheapest of all toys ;
They roll thee up, they toss thy ball about,
   A very joy of joys,
      Benignant snow !

So, shed o'er all the city—fresh from God—
   Thy pure and holy calm ;
Only the mammonite or senseless clod
   Will find no blessèd balm
      In winter's snow.

THE CREAKING DOOR.

Y chamber hath a creaking door,
    A window broad and high ;
    And from my pillow I watch the
      birds
    As they flit across the sky,
    Or perch on their nests in the
      ivy screen
    That hides and drapes the pro-
      jecting wall ;
    Though centuries old it is fresh
      and green,
    And has mounted o'er parapet,
      chimney, and all.—
    I lie in the languor of listless
      ease,
    When pain has wearied itself and
      me,
And clouds, and wings, and nodding trees,
Are all the life I care to see :—

True, the house is lofty, my chamber high,
  And I see but the tops of the tallest trees ;
But 'tis a luxury so to lie
  And watch them bend to the breath of the breeze ;
Mark the tremulous leaves, and the fluttering wings,
And the clouds, those changing, unchangeable things ;
Motion, just of that undulant kind—
It blends with the mood of the dormant mind,
Ere the grip of pain comes again to rouse
The writhing limbs, and the throbbing brows.

Then crimson sunsets fire the west,
  Grey cloudlets purple into black,
Birds fly for shelter to the nest,
  And I perchance am on the rack :
And when subsides my passing pain
Wild winds come tearing o'er the plain :
Wild winds that howl, and shriek, and rive,
  Like demons greedy for their prey,
Against the glass the tempest drive
  And through each cranny force their way ;
They drag the ivy from the wall,
  And with its tendrils lash the panes ;
In mockery to the clouds they call,
  And, answered back with pelting rains,
They sob, and moan, and hiss, and cry,
Like fiends in dire extremity.

Soon as these stormy winds arouse
  To chill the timid soul with dread,
Strange voices fill the large old house :—
  But I lie passive on my bed,
While unseen footsteps cross the floor,
And unseen fingers try the door,
Which opes not, though it sways and creaks,
  And creaks and sways, and creaks again,
With every blast that howls and shrieks,
Until I deem some spirit speaks
  In that same weird unearthly strain ;
And lie and listen, awe-struck, pale,
Till the voice dies, as dies the gale.

Yet captive to that painful couch
  Whilst moons and seasons wax and wane,
So long I watch the changing skies,
So oft I hear the storm-wind rise,
  So oft the creaking door's refrain,
I cease to shudder or to crouch
In listening to its undertones :—
For as the old door creaks and groans
  It tells me stories of the past ;
And calls up shadows from the tomb
To flit before me in the gloom,
Crowding with ghosts that panelled room,
  Evoked from darkness and the blast.

And, as the door throbs out and in
('Tis one of the few without a twin),
I learn why that barrier lost its mate,
And moans for its fellow early and late.

The house had been built in those perilous days
When 'twas neither safe to pray nor to praise,
Unless the prayer and the praise were given
To the very antithesis of Heaven ;
And lest servants should hear what their betters said,
In times when a whisper might cost a head,
It was only safe to have double doors,
And hiding places in walls and floors,
And provide the chambers with entrances twain
That whoso was in might get out again.

So, the spacious chamber wherein I lie
(With nervously sensitive ear and eye)
Had for entrance and exit just two such pairs,
One to a room, and one out to the stairs,
Or rather, unto a broad plateau
Whence the staircase leads, above and below ;
An ante-room surrounded by doors,
Shut off by *one* from the downward floors,
But open unto the floor above,—
Fit loitering place for hate or—love.

Till the chamber door, which was one of the pair
Abutting close on the downward stair,
  Failing a maiden at sorest need,
Was torn with a wrench from hinge and hasp,
Leaving its lonely partner to gasp
  And groan for aye o'er a darksome deed.

When Oliver Cromwell lived over the road
Old Joshua Coburn here abode,
  And they called each other "friend;"
But when Cromwell mounted the steps to the throne,
Joshua wisely kept to his own,
  And muttered, "Look to the end."
So when Charles the Second was king of the land,
And plots fed plots on every hand,
Joshua, secure as a grey old rock,
Only crumbled beneath the shock
Of seething, surging political waves
That swept so many brave men to their graves.
And, just as free from ambition's fire,
The puritan son of that puritan sire
  Held the house, and the lands around,
When the merry monarch had done with mirth,
And gone the way of *un*common earth,
  And James his brother was crowned.

Like to his father in all but his name
Oliver Coburn kept out of the flame,

And might have lived as serene a life,
Blest in his fortune, and blest in his wife,
But *he* had a son who was not so meek
As to offer the smiter, a second cheek ;
Who could not sit still and twiddle his thumbs
When.he heard the clamorous beat of drums ;
Nor let the sword girt on his manly thigh
Rust in its scabbard ingloriously :
Whose pulses beat an impetuous tune,
Warm as the air in the flushing of June :
Whose spirit chafed in the fireside nook
As waters chafe in a mountain brook ;
Longing for action and wider space
For the soul to move, the life to race :
Who had a liking for feathers and lace,
    For velvet doublets, and jewels rare ;
Could lift his hat, with a courtly grace,
    And scrupled to crop his curling hair :
With an eye for colour, an ear for sound,
And feet that tingled to join in a round ;
And, casting the slough of his sober suit,
To follow the lead of pipe or lute
Where women were fair, and men were brave,
And hands might clasp round the glass or the glaive.

But though, like a fluttering bird in a net,
Did the active soul of Mark Coburn fret
To escape from the narrow bounds of home,
He cared not to journey so far as Rome ;

For the Coburn creed was no slipshod thing ;
In the metal of Mark was no spurious ring,
And he could not kneel to the popish king.

So he nurtured thoughts in his seething brain,
That boded ill for the monarch's reign—
If to plan and to do were the self-same thing,
And all men agreed in their choice of a king.—
He knitted his brows, and he pattered his feet,
As he moodily mused on a garden seat ;
Or he joined the household meal, and prayer,
With mind astray, and a vacant air.
Yet not e'en his sister Priscilla knew
Whither the dreams of her brother flew,
Though she watched with the anxious eye of love,
And the timid heart of a fearful dove ;
Deeming his evident lapse from grace
Caused by some wicked and winsome face.
And she pondered late, and she pondered long,
How a maiden might right so grave a wrong.

Soon there came a day
When Mark rode away,
With his hidden heart elate ;
Ripe for what fray
Should come in his way,
And reckless of adverse fate.

Ere he crossed his steed the die was cast ;—
  Yet never a word to sister or sire,
Of the purpose which lit his eye with fire,
  Spake he to the very last.

  " Better he grieve for an errant son
    Than suffer for deed of mine."
  It was kindly meant—but evil *done*
    Snaps the best *intention's* line,
  And few discern what a coil is spun
    When deceit begins to twine.

Priscilla was sad, she knew not why,
  And the father was loth to let him go,
As Mark grasped each hand with a grave good-bye,
  And turned his back on the house at Bow.
He had gone for a sojourn—so they thought—
With their godly kinsman Ephraim Short ;
And Oliver deemed that good man's care,
His exhortations and pious prayer,
Might steady his somewhat wayward heir.

Alack, for peaceful Oliver's hope !
  Good Ephraim Short salutes no guest.—
Mark Coburn's aims have wider scope ;
  He seeks bold Monmouth in the west !

With sword on thigh, and spurs to steed,
He follows close Lord Shrewsbury's lead ;
And riding fast, and riding late,
With pauses few to rest and bait,
In loyal Taunton draws his rein,
'Mid martial sight and martial strain,
To feed his eyes and ears with all
That can his sanguine soul enthral.
He hears the herald's voice proclaim
    James Monmouth England's king;
    The people's deafening acclaim
        Through the blue welkin ring :
He sees the fair maids of the town
Kneel at the new-made monarch's feet, ·
    Who flings his small chance of the crown
Away on pageant in the street,
When he should gather, as he goes,
The force to meet onrushing foes.
    Ah ! fatal, impotent delay !
To waste the time in silken show,
    When Feversham is on the way,
With troops that come as billows flow !

Now, fiery hot, on Sedgemoor's plain
They met—who ne'er would meet again;
And far and fast the orders ran,
"To arms ! to horse ! each youth and man !"

Then harquebus, and pike, and sword,
In the fierce contest, gashed and gored.
And,—warlike son of peaceful sires,—
'Mid flashing steel and flashing fires,
Once having fleshed his maiden blade,
Mark's arm grew stiff ere it was stayed.

Hark ! Cries of " Treason !" on the wind
Scared from the contest lord and hind !
The dastard duke, for whom men gave ·
Life's free-will offering to the glaive,
For whom they chivalrously fought,
Had basely fled ! *Their* lives were nought !
What recked he that his followers bled,
So he preserved *his* royal head !

Swift through the ranks the rumour ran :—
   Was *such* the tinselled thing
They had mistaken for a man
   Fit to be crowned a king ?
Young Valour, sickened at the core,
Turned in its shame, to fight no more ;
Old Honour flung its weapon down,
Too proud to strike for such a crown ;
Nay, shame disarmed the roughest lout
Who heard the foe's derisive shout ;

Scorn put the fire of battle out,
And slaughter revelled in a rout.

Mark Coburn scarce could know or tell
Whether he fought or ill or well,
So fiery fierce the bloody fight :
    With snort of steed, and clash of steel,
So desperate the hurried flight,
    With swift pursuers at his heel.
But on; and on, he kept his course,
Still urging on his flagging horse,
Till by a fordless river's brim
The panting steed refused to swim.

Promptly the reins were cast aside :—
Mark flung himself into the tide
Accoutred though he happed to be.
A fearless swimmer of the Lea,
He hailed the current as a friend
It had pleased Providence to send ;—
And so, the Parret's buoyant breast
Floated him swiftly unto rest
Far from the doubtful haunts of men,
Beyond the grim pursuer's ken,
Beyond the sound of raging strife,
Exhausted, wounded, but with life :
And life has charms when years are few,
E'en though its wine hold dregs of rue.

M

He found safe shelter in a nook,
　Where trees were thick, and shadows dense,
And a lone hut beside a brook
　Held charity without pretence.
Seldom might stranger foot intrude
Within that sylvan solitude,
Where a poor woodman, rude of speech,
Proved kindly host and skilful leech,
Aye ready to resign, or share,
His bracken bed, his homely fare,
Though only the Adamite brotherhood
Linked him of the world with him of the wood.

＊　　＊　　＊　　＊　　＊

What hath come over the house at Bow?
The truant returns not, and time is slow!
　Old Oliver mourns for his missing son,
And aimlessly wanders to and fro,
　Mutely questioning clock and the sun.
For rumour has flown on the wing of the wind,
And sown its seed in the Coburn mind.
But doubt never grows to the ear of truth;
Or stern displeasure would banish ruth:
For Oliver pictures his son waylaid,
And, plundered by rogues who make crime a trade,
Left to die in some lonely Epping brake,—
Or, gone astray for some maiden's sake;
But that son of *his* should dash into strife,
To give a zest and colour to life!—

That son of *his* should have plotted and schemed,
The good man neither suspected nor dreamed.
Yet when whispers of "treason" reach his ear
His heart is stirred by a nameless fear,
And the still house echoes his restless tread,
As hope grows faint, and dies in dread.

E'en pale Priscilla hath paler grown !
Her voice hath a strange, abstracted tone,
As she goes about her household ways,
Or joins in the daily prayer and praise,
Or idly sits with folded hands,
Or briefly issues her grave commands.;
And, ever and aye, her head is bent
As if with listening ear intent.
    And then she will start
    With a sinking heart ;
And. then, with a weary sigh of relief,
Cast off some load of fear or grief.
But rarely a word, from day to day,
Breathes she of him who has gone away.
And never a hint of doubt, or blame,
Falls from her lips on her brother's name,—
From that hour, when in secret, after dark,
She let in a fugitive, like unto Mark,
With never a whisper to servant or sire ;
Lest the doom of the household be swift and dire.

She looks on her father with pitiful eyes—·
    Eyes that are brimming to overflow,
But she dares not cast off her heart's disguise,
    Lest she add afresh to that old man's woe.
So Oliver prays for his son's return,
Prays daily the truth of his fate to learn ;
Whilst over the house doth mystery creep,
As though phantoms walk whilst the inmates sleep.

But who are these at the outer gate,
Thundering loudly—who will not wait ?
Who are these ruffians that entrance claim
By the potent spell of the monarch's name
    (While Priscilla swift up the staircase flits) ;
Who come with a swagger, and clash of steel,
The morioned head and the iron heel,—
And, thrusting old Dorothy aside,
Stalk through the hall with braggart stride,
    To the room where Oliver Coburn sits ?

Comrades, these, of the "lambs" of Kirke,
All fresh from Taunton's tragic work ;
Come,—with their glances loose and free,
And language tainted with ribaldry,—
To question the maid, and the grey-haired man,
    Of the missing brother and son,

And every nook in the house to scan,
  Where even a rat might run.
Whilst Oliver Coburn stands aghast,
Startled as by a trumpet-blast,
Stunned by the ruthless charge they bear,
To seek a traitor hiding there.

" What ! Mark be that attainted thing,
A rebel armed against his king ! "
He answers them with rising scorn :
" No treason on *this* hearth was born !
Here lurks no rebel from Sedgemoor !
The Coburn loyalty is sure !
Search, an ye will, from ground to roof—
My father's home will stand the proof ! "

Priscilla's close-shut lips are white,
Her bosom pants with new affright,
She hears, yet nerves herself to stand
Unflinchingly before that band
Of fierce, ferocious, lawless men,—
Like wolves let loose from some foul den,—
Who mock the sanctity of home,
And boldly o'er the mansion roam,
To test the panels, probe the beds,
Mount from the cellars to the leads,
Peer into closets, open chests,
Heedless who murmurs—who protests ;

Not even the maiden's dainty nest
Sacred from their unhallowed quest.
And, wherever they go, there is clamour and clang,
And doors are opened and shut with a bang,
And riot is master, where peace was lord,
Riot that comes where the law is the sword.

To the broad plateau by her chamber door
    Priscilla has followed with frightened feet ;
And sees them ascend to the attic floor,
    While her heart and her pulses cease to beat.
She knows what lies where the ceiling dips
    O'er the landing, midway up that attic stair ;
She knows, how in grooves a frame-work slips
    Where the corner tiles have a sun-red glare ;
Tiles that glide upward with scarce a sound,
    Under their fellows, that overlap ;
And she dreads, lest the nook that was never found,
    Instead of a covert should prove a trap.—
She hears a trooper unlock the door,
    The little door to the roof and sky,
˙And she hears his boots go clattering o'er
    The tiles, where her heart and her secret lie.
She hears a curse from his lips profane,—
Sees—something darken the window-pane ;
Hears an awful shriek, a more awful thud—
The trooper lies dead in his own bad blood !

Dead—far down on the stones below—
Where the sentry, pacing to and fro,
Answers the shriek with a shriek and a groan,
Though his heart is hard as that reddened stone.
(A rebel to kill may be right enough
But a comrade is made of different stuff.)

Priscilla—she knows not what, or whom,
O'er that parapet low has gone to his doom ;
But her lips and cheeks are blanched as her brow,
   Her brow where she presses her thin white hand,
As the tumult that rises upward now,
   Deprives her limbs of the power to stand.

There are rough feet racing up the stair :—
A moment her pale lips move in prayer—
She would hide in her chamber, did she dare,
But ransacking foes she can hear within :
   Still, it is perilous there to stay
And face the troop, coming with ireful din.
   An instant—and she has slipped away,—
Concealed from both by the double doors ;
Whilst, surging up, as a billow roars,
Four or five soldiers rush to the roof,
Eager all to put to the proof,
Whether their comrade's broken crown
   Was due to a slip, or the rebel's hand,

To a dizzy brain on looking down,
　Or a struggle where Mark had firmer stand.
And between the doors, with bated breath
Priscilla listens—for life or death.

Cautiously creeping, like beasts of prey,
They circuit the roof as best as they may,
But never a sign of man or mouse,
Find they on the tiles of the tall old house.

So, cursing the " nonconformist dog,"
　And cursing that rebel Mark,
Wishing 'twas he that lay like a log—
　Not their comrade cold and stark,
Growling, they creep through the little door,
And shamble back to the lower floor,
Leaving one of their band behind
To ponder the chances of seek and find.

And he casts a swift and searching glance
O'er the river, and marshes' wild expanse,
Wide spread in the rear of the house at Bow;
Where a flying figure must surely show.
Then, as one who would ferret a secret out,
　His keen eyes traverse the rise of roof;
And he mutters words that imply a doubt
　To be resolved by a speedy proof;

And rising, the better to have a look
  How far it is down from that parapet wall,
By chance he stands close to the hidden nook,
  As he marvels how Roger happened to fall,
When, silently, up slide the corner tiles,
  Two muscular hands his ankles grip
And over the parapet topples Miles,
  Just as his comrade chanced to trip.

Again, through the air rings despair's wild cry;
  Again there's a crash on the crimsoned stones,
And something lies there makes no reply,
  Though the captain calls in his sharpest tones !
In blankest horror these pitiless men
  Look each unto each in amaze and dread ;
Then skyward up at the dwelling—and then
  Glance downward to scan the disfigured dead ;
Perplexed inquiry on each hard face :
  Who will *this mystery* dare to trace ?

But grouping round that garden door,
  Stand none with aspect so dismayed
As Oliver, on whose peaceful floor
  The curse of blood for aye is laid.
He clasps his quivering hands, to gaze
  With starting eyes and lips apart,

As one whom horror seems to daze,—
  A revelation in his heart !

A moment's pause—the air is rent
  With angry shouts and curses dire ;
And savage impulse finds a vent
  In vengeful threats 'gainst maid and sire.
But as they seize the grey-haired man
  To answer for—they know not what,
Save that his son is under ban,
  Through the old homestead rings a shot !
A shot—a woman's piercing scream ;
  And then a tumult on the stair,
And then—does Oliver doat or dream ?—
  "Help ! help !" *Mark's* voice is calling there ;
" Help, here !" above the clash of swords ;
  And serving-men rush up to aid ;
But close upon those frantic words,
  Young Mark, o'erpowered, in death is laid.

Sad sight for Oliver Coburn's eyes !
  His missing son has come to light.
But, oh ! the anguish of surprise,
  Day suddenly eclipsed by night.
Alack ! that ever he was born !
  That son lies gashed upon the floor,

And—ne'er was a father more forlorn !—
Prostrate against a splintered door
His darling, his Priscilla cast,
(Like a leaf driven by the blast),
With closèd lids, and pallid lips
　　Deserted by life's ebbing tide,
Which from the shoulder slowly drips
　　To join the large red pool beside.

A fine old man, erect and firm,
　　Was Oliver two short hours agone ;
But now—he seems a shrinking worm
　　That Fate has put its foot upon ;
So crushed by the o'erwhelming shock,
He hears nor jibe, nor taunt, nor mock.

Nor does he hear yon braggart tell
His fellows how it all befell ;
How he and Gilbert, lying pent
Within that room, were on the scent ;
Or how himself and his brave mate,
The ready servants of the state,
Heard a spy breathing by the door,
And thought a shot might clear the score.
" 'Twas that white witch who played the spy,
Couched 'twixt the doors secure and sly,

And 'twas her screech that brought the whelp
Out from his kennel, bawling ' Help !'
So I and Gilbert to it fell ;
And think ye not *we helped* him well?"
Hark ! how they laugh at the man's rude jest,
In brutal comment on fatal quest,
As down they go for a free carouse,
Before they vacate the Coburn house,
Before they carry their dead away,
Or "suffer the rebel at home to stay !"

Old Dorothy creeps to her master's side,
    When they leave him alone with *his* dead ;
But she sees that his eyes are fixed and wide,
    As one from whom sense hath fled.
" Alack !" cries she, " for this woful day !
    The Lord hath smitten his servant sore !"
And she fain would lead his steps away,
    From the sorry sight on the oaken floor.

With tender touch, and tearful eyes,
    They raise Priscilla's senseless form,
And lo ! the maiden faintly sighs,
    The wound still bleeds, the breath is warm.

"See, master, see, Priscilla lives :
    One prop is left for thine old age !"

No sign the stricken father gives,—
His mind is yet a vacant page.
But when the place of foes is clear,—
The splintered door is torn away,
To make a temporary bier,
For young Mark Coburn's stiffened clay,—
Then, a dim glimmering of light
Dawns on the old man's darkened sight,
And from his lips, prolonged and low,
Breaks forth a wail of utter woe—
The feeble, helpless, hopeless cry
Of childish imbecility.

The house was spared all further raid :
And, when King William filled the throne,
Sole mistress was a white-faced maid
Who dwelt unwedded there alone.
Not long, the broken-hearted sire,
With trembling limbs and mind astray,
Had kept his place beside the fire,
To hold her hand the livelong day :
Alone, with bloodless lip and cheek,
That never warmed with blush or smile,
Priscilla Coburn, grave and meek,
Sat kinless in the mournful pile.
Yet not unsought, although unwed ;
Brave suitors came, but none might stay :

Her heart was with the buried dead,
  Her hand too cold to give away.
She ne'er replaced the riven door;
Ne'er trod again that upper floor,
  With her loved brother's blood imbrued;
Nor could she cross the garden stones,
Lest she should hear those troopers' groans—
So much that day her life imbued.

It closed her hand to wedded touch,
But opened it to all in need;
The Master's tender "Inasmuch"
Became her guide, her law, her creed.
And when Priscilla's thread was spun,
And angels hailed her with "Well done!"
Her angel-work was but begun:
For countless children, poor, forlorn,
  Have blessed Priscilla Coburn's Will,
And countless children yet unborn
  Might bless their benefactress still
Had her gift been conserved with Charity's zeal
And faithful regard for such "little ones'" weal.

And this is the story the creaking door
  Told me as it mourned for its wooden twin.
If it lied—so has *history* lied before;
  And the legend should have some truth therein,

For Priscilla's Will remains to this day
Though the "Coburn Charity" dwindles away,
And the schools she endowed with fair dwellings and land
Have been built upon trusts scarcely safer than sand :
Yet the land has not vanished, or lessened in worth,
And the houses have still a firm foothold on earth.

Hist ! the door creaks like a sentient thing—
Man can pluck the plumes from an angel's wing !

UNDER A SPELL.

"WHAT doest thou there, oh! thou maiden so
    fair,
    By the brink of this woodland well?"
"I know not, Sir Knight, I can answer aright,
  I fear I am under a spell.

"Two nights and two days I have trod tangled ways
    Towards a fountain beheld in a dream,
Thro' brake and thro' briar, thro' mud and thro' mire,
    Drawn hither—for this is the stream."

"So young and so fair, hadst thou never a care
    For the dangers of forest and fell,
For foul beasts of prey, or men fouler than they,
    That thou seekest the Whispering Well?"

"I know not, Sir Knight, but I tell thee aright,
  And fear I am under a spell; .
From a dream I arose, donned my kirtle and hose,
  To seek out this mystical well.

"I came by constraint, if of fiend or of saint
  I know not—I only can tell,
Without pause I have prest to the end of my quest,
  This musical, fern-shaded well."

"Was there never a sire, a page or esquire,
  To guard thee for love or for fee,
That thou strayest at large with thy honour in charge,
  And beauty to tempt—even me?"

"Sir Knight, I've a sire, have page and esquire;
  They slept while the portals flew wide;
The warders I past with all senses bound fast,
  Nor knew I of harm to betide."

"Now speakest thou truth? or, art cunning forsooth,
  And of beauty a little too free?
Say, what was the dream brought a maid to this stream,
  Was it love, or diablerie?"

N

"Sir Knight, by my tears, by my fast coming fears,
   I feel I am bound by a spell;
By no will of my own I came hither alone
   To muse by this murmuring well.

"I saw in a dream a spring feeding a stream,
   With forest trees arching o'erhead;
I bent low to the brink, but ere I could drink
   A voice called me—and hither I fled:

"Fled through forest and glade, in sunshine and shade,
   Fleet-footed o'er pathways unknown,
That voice in my ear ringing fatefully clear—
   'Come, Bertha—I wait thee, mine own.'

"I know not, Sir Knight, that I tell thee aright,
   Or if I yet waken or dream :—
The voice had a tone, oh! so much like thine own!
   Didst *thou* call my soul to this stream?"

"*I* called thee not, maid; but I slept 'neath this shade,
   And drank of this mystical spring.
See, it ebbs and it flows, it comes and it goes
   Like thy blushes, thou beautiful thing.

" I dared the weird fay of the fountain to lay
  Love's spell on *my* immobile heart ;
So drank of the stream—and I, too, had a dream ;
  And thou of my dream wert a part.

" As the spring ebbs and flows, so my hopes sank and rose
  As I saw thee, sweet, hasting this way ;
Though I knew not thy name, or whither thou came,
  I knew thou wert brought by the fay.

" Still, loth to resign what heart-freedom was mine,
  I tried thee, with doubt in my breath :
Thy fearful replies and immaculate eyes
  Have bound me thy slave unto death."

" I know not, Sir Knight, if I hear thee aright,
  I feel I am under a spell ;
I shrink from thy glance, yet I long to advance—
  Ah ! what says the Whispering Well ? "

" Stoop, Bertha, and drink ; I am up to the brink,
  I ebb if thou tarriest long :
Thy knight had quaffed deep when I lulled him to sleep,
  With *thee* for the theme of my song.

" His soul called to thine from my mystical shrine,
    Thou camest, so potent the spell ;
Now he looks for thy love all earth's blessings above ;
    So drink thou of my magical well.

" Bend thy lips to my brim—Soh ! thou turnest to him—
    Thou'st drank of thy fate at the flood ! "
" Oh ! Bertha, mine own ; thou cam'st hither alone—
    I'll guard thee henceforth through life's wood."

THE GREY MONK'S "MISERERE."

THE grey monk patters a midnight prayer—
    "Miserere Domine !"
      Along the corridor, down the stair,
  A light foot creepeth stealthily.
Pausing, he crosses himself in dread
  (Never a footstep there should be)
As near his cell comes that stealthy tread
  At the midnight hour so warily.

The grey monk mutters, in gasping prayer,
    "Miserere Domine !"
When the step that comes adown the stair
  Stops at his door familiarly.
His rigid face is grey as his gown
  (A ruddy face it is wont to be),
From his trembling hands the beads drop down
  As the door flies open readily.

The grey monk shudders, but not with the cold,
  (He has bethought what this may be),
As wrapped in many a muffling fold
  A figure enters solemnly.
His terrified heart emits the groan,
  " Miserere Domine ! "
For closer yet, without sign or tone,
  The shape approaches steadily.

The grey monk's brain has begun to swim,
  Flooded o'er by memory,—
The guilt of his life comes home to him
  In one fell swoop portentously.
Well he remembers that muffled form,
  Veiled and voiceless though it be,
Erewhile a woman young and warm—
  Now, a spectral mystery.

The grey monk shrinks as an icy hand,
  Pulseless as a polar sea,
Laid on his wrist in stern command
  Draws him from his bended knee ;
Draws him slowly from out his cell,
  Powerless to resist or flee,
Whilst overhead the midnight bell
  Breaks the silence eerily.

The grey monk follows through cloistered gloom,
  (Miserere Domine !),
Palsied as by a sense of doom
  And perpetual misery ;
Follows the phantom through secret ways
  Never planned by piety
But trodden oft in amorous days,
  Trodden once so murd'rously.

The dark trees shudder as on they pass,
  The tearful dew drops dolefully,
A low moan comes from the conscious grass,
  The gusty wind sobs humanly ;
The phantom stops at an eerie nook,
  Black and gruesome as can be,
Where even the moonbeams fear to look
  On the grey monk crouching piteously.

Down, close by the deep pool's oozy edge,
  Pool as still as death must be,
The grey monk kneels, amid weed and sedge,
  A wretch in mortal agony :
The spectral finger points to the pool,—
  Be it fact or phantasy,
He sees a sight of dolour and doole—
  Glares, and shrieks despairingly.

An upturned face looks out from the slime,
   Fair as face of maid might be,
A silent witness of secret crime,
   Double sin and treachery;
Looks, as the drownèd dead *can* look,
   In his eyes reproachingly :—
The murderer reads, as from written book,
   The awful doom he yet must dree.

A gracious year for remorse has gone
   To the past's immutability,
Since on the Eve of the good St. John
   A soul went to eternity;
Sent all unshriven to God's white throne
   Full of sin as we may be,
No single moment spared to atone,—
   So she went—accusingly.

Over the fate of the missing maid
   Hung a pall of mystery;
But the grey monk felt no whit afraid,
   Still secure in sanctity.
He never confessed the hideous spot
   Tainting his soul like leprosy;—
Forgot his guilt,—but the Judge did not—
   Doom comes sure if silently.

Never again will he *patter* the prayer
" Miserere Domine ! "
He wails it out to the midnight air,
And echoes mock his misery.
For when comes round the Eve of St. John,
Phantom led, in agony,
That face in the pool he must gaze upon
Till time becomes eternity.

THE OWL'S FLIGHT.

U whit, tu whoo !
    The fluffy owl hath taken its flight
    By the lady's stair at deep midnight,
Down to the gloomy wood below,
Where the restless trees toss to and fro,
Back to her nest on the ivied wall,
Where by night or day dark shadows fall.

    Tu whit, tu whoo !
The owl's grey wings in the clear moonlight
Mark out the line of a sadder flight,
When banners of flame waved in the breeze,
And ruddied the tops of the shrinking trees,
When the castle was given to fire and sword,
And the savage will of a despot's horde.

    Tu whit, tu whoo !
All sights and sounds that filled the air
Were of havoc, slaughter, and despair

The clash of weapons, the shriek of pain,
The victors' shout o'er the ghastly slain,
As tongues of flame licked up the gore
That ran in streams on each oaken floor.

Tu whit, tu whoo !
With a gash cleft through both helm and brain,
Sir Hubert lay soulless among the slain :
His lady, but in her night robe drest,
Fled, with their infant clasped to her breast,
By a steep and rock-built outer stair,
For refuge and safety—anywhere.

Tu whit, tu whoo !
The night was chilly—she felt it not,
Her lips were parched, her heart was hot ;
She *must* preserve her darling's life,
And her own fair fame as Hubert's wife !
Down the steep stairway she flashed like light,
Gained the dark wood and was lost to sight.

Tu whit, tu whoo !
Alas ! the fiends were on her track :
Childless, they drove the mother back,
Goading her on with wanton spears,
And brutal jests that taint her ears :
She heard her doom—their leader's prey,—
She must escape it—how she may !

Tu whit, tu whoo !
The precipice is sheer and steep,
No life could bear the downward leap.
She paused anigh to the topmost stair,
Paused in her madness and blank despair ;
They taunted her with lack of breath,—
One bound—she had escaped—*to death !*

" Tu whit, tu whoo ! "
Screeches the night owl.   Moonlight falls
On blackened ruins and crumbling walls.
And ever thus through the midnight air
It wings its flight by that fatal stair ;
And 'tis said that owl is the lady's ghost,
Shrieking—while seeking the babe she lost.

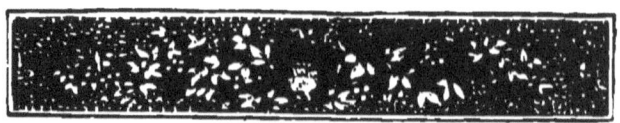

THE LADY'S LANE.

(A LEGEND OF THE LONG-AGO.)

Manville abounds in specimens of the cool and shady *cavée*, the most beautiful and sequestered of which bears the name of Cavée de la Dame. Tradition, which has kept the name, has forgotten to give it a meaning. This Lady's Cavée is a deep, dark, winding path, lonely and mysterious, a spot much frequented by blackbirds and lovers in spring. Trees grow on either side its steep banks, and they are ages old, says tradition.—MISS JULIA KAVANNAH.

A STILL, sequestered, winding lane,
  (Normandy holds many such),
  Where neither summer sun, nor rain,
Penetrateth overmuch ;
Where o'er the steep and ferny banks
  Sombre crests of ancient trees
Stand up erect in serried ranks,
  And scarce do homage to the breeze
That sways their branches to and fro,
As trembling leaves are whisp'ring low
Dread secrets of the long-ago. .

A lichen-covered, grey old stone,
   There since days of Charlemagne,
With not an ear for sigh or moan,
   Not a pulse for joy or pain ;
Yet, gruesome witness of the past,
   Stained for aye by deed most foul,
Far deeper shadows it o'ercast
   Than of bat or flitting owl ;
For nightly paces to and fro
A lovely lady white with woe,—
A phantom of the long-ago.

A lady, marvellously fair,
   In her eyes love's tender light,
Baffling her warder's watchful care,
   Hither came to meet her knight :
Came, with the midnight for a veil,
   And no escort but a page,
To hear the oft-repeated tale
   Young lips tell from age to age—
Sweet murmured words, so faint and low
They cheat the echoes as they flow,—
Love-whispers of the long-ago.

A deadly feud 'tween sire and sire
   Interposed to bar their bliss ;
Nay more—a jealous rival's ire
   Made it crime her glove to kiss ;

And so, in secret oft they met,
  Trusting maid, enamoured knight;
While perils which the path beset
  Deepened, if subdued, delight;
As, with hearts and cheeks aglow,
Entranced they wandered to and fro,
Young lovers of the long-ago.

Alas! they once too oft kept tryst—
  Treachery had kept it too:
Only the moon those pale lips kissed,
  Only winds sighed love's adieu!
Slain—even on the trysting stone,—
  Bathed in gore the true knight lay;
She, with no voice to shriek or moan,
  Palsied stood till torn away:
Then the blank stillness of her woe
Broke into wailings sad and low—
But heard in heaven—long ago.

At feast or tournay nevermore
  Shone that lady 'mid her peers;
But midnight found her, as of yore,
  Keeping tryst through vacant years:
Not even death could break the spell,
  Love was stronger in its pain,

And where her Bertrand bleeding fell
  Her spirit haunts the darksome lane;
Still slowly pacing to and fro,
As gusty shadows come and go,—
A spectre of the long-ago.

We call it yet the Lady's Lane
  Though centuries have passed away;
And lovers—God defend the twain !—
  Idly by this stone will stray.
Tradition may forget the tale,
  Lichens gather on the stone,
Men see no phantom, wan and pale,
  Flit around it with a moan,
Yet still she wanders to and fro
When midnight shadows come and go,—
A memory of the long-ago.

THE DRUID'S OAK.

"**B**EWARE!"—thus an aged sibyl spoke—
"The fateful path by the Druid's Oak,
The kiss of love and the vengeful stroke.

"Beware of tryst 'neath the Druid's tree,
With the simple maid of low degree,
When the pulses beat too rapidly.

"Beware the sting of a broken troth;
Both sweet and bitter must be for *both;*
And a maiden frail makes strong men wroth.

"Mark well, Sir Guy, on thy bridal eve
If the red wine stain thy lady's sleeve;
For by that dark token will she grieve.

"Sure portent that of the coming crash
'Neath the growing oak, from riven ash,
And of red rain falling with a splash.

"'Ware, then, thou quit not thy lady's side
Till the marriage knot be truly tied
And thy doom by prayer be set aside.

" Beware, Sir Guy, lest it fall to thee
To dree the weird of the Druid's tree,
Life-blood must pay for love-perjury ! "

He'd crossed her hand with a silver crown,
Yet now he cried, with a hasty frown,
" I'll have thee whipt through the market-town ! "

He raised his whip from his horse's flank :
The aged crone neither stirred nor shrank,
Save to lift a finger, lean and lank.

" Ay, whip thou the prophetess of ill ?
Whip, but despise not the sibyl's skill,
Lest time her auguries dark fulfil ! "

Sir Guy had been long across the sea,
And courted and kissed 'neath many a tree
And laughed at the gipsy's augury.

" Pshaw ! It is I am the most to blame,
Giving my coin and ear to the dame !"
And he rode off lightly as he came.

Had he forgotten the day and hour
He kissed the bloom from a sweet wild flower,
And left it to droop in wind and shower?

Had he forgotten the kith and kin
Of the cottage maiden lured to sin,
Or the woodland depths he then was in?

" Curse the old hag and her witchery !
This rugged oak is the self-same tree
That heard my whispers to Marjory !

" Ah, well, 'twas but an error of youth,
An episode in a life forsooth !
For now I love with a truer truth."

He spurred the sides of his loit'ring steed,
With small remorse for the selfish deed,
That left his victim to shame and need.

Nay, with a glow of enamoured pride,
Sir Guy sped onward to clasp his bride,
And vow a love that should aye abide.

" Wilt bind thy vow 'neath the Druid's tree,"
Quoth his fair young bride right saucily,
" (As thou vowed to hapless Marjory) ? "

Was that a voice in his ear or brain ?—
The wine from his glass is spilt like rain—
The lady's robe has a crimson stain.

Her cheek grows red as his lip turns white :
" Sir Guy, you are somewhat strange to-night ! "
" Dearest, I tremble with my delight."

He lingers long by his dear one's side ;—
" Sir Guy, 'tis late ; you have far to ride ! "
Shall he tell the omen, and abide ?

" Pshaw ! shall I blanch on my bridal eve
At a spot of wine on my lady's sleeve
For fictions a gipsy chose to weave ? "

Hush ! who are those by the Druid's tree,
Who crouch and creep so warily ?
Are they aught akin to Marjory ?

THE DRUID'S OAK.

The woods to-night have an aspect grim,
The moaning wind sings a dirge to him,
And his good steed quivers in every limb.

Yet rashly Sir Guy pursues his track,
Though every branch seems to wave him back,
And o'er the moon sweeps a cloudy rack.

He nears the spot he was bade " Beware ! "
Has never Sir Guy one word of prayer
To touch the heart of one listener there ?

'Neath the Druid's Oak, the riven ash
Comes down with a sudden thud and crash,
And red rain spurts from many a gash.

Alack ! for the swift sharp agony
That tells the weird he is doomed to dree,
For kissing false 'neath the mystic tree.

His steed is gone with a start and bound,
His throat is torn by the springing hound,
Three bludgeons batter him to the ground.

Three men have sinned for his light sin's sake,
Whose bridal-bed is the tangled brake,
Kissed by the toad and clasped by the snake.

And long will the moon sad silence keep,
Though the mournful clouds bow down and weep,
O'er that ghastly, dread, unending sleep.

PRINTED AT THE CAXTON PRESS, BECCLES.